SWEET DADDY'S FUNERAL

SHANI SMITH

DEDICATION

*This book is dedicated in loving memory of my father,
James Melvin Smith.*

*In addition, this book is dedicated to
all fathers who do their best to support their families.*

ONE

1994

Kema is a "Daddy's Girl," her father, Benjamin's pride and joy. After work, he meets Kema at the bus stop to walk her home. At least three times a week he takes her to the corner store to buy her Sprite, Oreos, Blue Raspberry Airheads, and Doritos. He also purchases a bottle of St. Ides and a pack of Wrigley's spearmint gum for himself.

"Baby girl, how was your day?" Benjamin asks Kema after taking a quick drink from the bottle.

"It was good, Daddy. In math, we learned how to solve algebra equations. In social studies, we learned about how the first United States colony in Jamestown, Virginia, was established," Kema replies.

"It sounds like you learned a lot today. I'm proud of you. Now, what about recess? I hope you weren't kissing any boys behind the bleachers."

Kema laughs and tries not to choke on her Doritos before she replies. "No, Daddy. Boys are mean. I don't want to kiss them."

"That's right, boys are mean. Keep studying and when you are older, a good man like your Daddy will find you."

"Yes sir," Kema replies.

Kema eats her snacks while Benjamin drinks the bottle of St. Ides like it is water quenching his thirst. There is a crack in the sidewalk and Benjamin trips on it and stumbles.

"Daddy, do you need me to hold your hand?" Kema asks.

"Very funny, Baby girl. I'm alright." Benjamin reaches in his left pocket to get the gum.

After walking about half a block towards their home, Kema hides the snacks she didn't finish in her backpack. The only evidence of their trip to the corner store are the crumbs Benjamin forgot to brush off of her face. When Kema and Benjamin arrive home, they are welcomed by Janice looking crossly at them both. Kema smiles sheepishly at Janice as she braces for the inevitable admonishment.

"Ben, I told you to quit buying snacks for Kema at that raggedy store every day after school. It spoils her appetite for real food. If she keeps eating all that junk food, she will be as big as a house when she gets older."

"Kema will be alright. A few cookies and chips ain't gonna to hurt her. Maybe it's that so-called real food you have been cooking that will hurt her."

Benjamin turns and looks at Kema with a devilish grin knowing that he has successfully irritated Janice. Kema returns his smile and experiences the same satisfaction he is feeling.

Janice looks at Benjamin and Kema with playful disdain. "I see the two of you are teaming up on me, but I will get the last laugh. "Go wash your hands and face for dinner," Janice commands.

"Yes, ma'am", Benjamin and Kema reply in unison. Kema goes to the bathroom to wash her hands and face. Benjamin moves toward Janice and hugs her from behind as she is wiping the countertop.

Janice smiles, continues wiping the countertop, and says, "You always conveniently forget that I snagged you with my cooking Benjamin."

"It wasn't your cooking Janice. It was the way your hips were swaying from side to side when you brought me my food at the diner. I knew from that moment you could serve me anytime. . ."

"Watch your mouth, Ben, Kema is listening."

"It's not like she hasn't heard us talk like this before."

Janice releases herself from Benjamin's embrace and turns to face him. "I know, but you are pouring it on pretty thick this evening. Have you been drinking? You told me that you were going to stop drinking."

"Now don't start in on me, Janice. You know I have been stressed since they started talking about laying off the truck unloaders."

"Is drinking and buying Kema junk food going to help the situation? I told you I can pick up an extra shift at the diner. Mama said we can move back in with her if you get laid off."

"You have said that a million times, Janice. But I'm a man. We can't go running back to your Mama every time we are broke. I will figure something out. Let's just eat this real food of yours and talk about this later."

TWO

Kema knows something is wrong when she gets off the school bus at 3:00 p.m. and Benjamin is not there waiting for her. Sometimes Benjamin's bus from work is delayed ten to fifteen minutes. Benjamin told her that if he is not there to pick her up by 3:20 p.m., it is ok to walk half a block home. Kema waits for twenty minutes and then walks home. On the days that Kema and Benjamin don't stop at the corner store, it only takes ten minutes to walk home. Walking alone, the walk takes Kema twice as long. She keeps turning around to see if Benjamin is there trying to catch up with her. When Kema approaches the front door, she sees Janice who looks confused that Kema is walking alone.

"Your Daddy's bus must have run late?"

"Yeah, I guess . . ." replies Kema as she disappointedly slings her backpack from her shoulder and places it by the door.

"What's with the attitude? Your Daddy's bus has run late before. He will be home soon. Go change your clothes and start your homework."

"Yes ma'am."

Kema follows her mother's instructions. After doing her homework for thirty minutes at the kitchen table, she walks to the living room and looks out the window. Kema doesn't see Benjamin. Janice and Kema sit down for dinner an hour later. Kema does not have an appetite and rearranges the green peas and baked chicken on her plate as if moving them around in a certain order would make Benjamin magically appear.

"Kema, you are playing with your food again instead of eating."

"I'm not hungry, Mama, I can't eat unless Daddy is here."

Janice's stern face softens, and she replies: "I know. Give me your plate and I will wrap it up and place it in the refrigerator for you to eat tomorrow. You should finish your homework, and by the time you finish, I'm sure your Daddy will be here."

"Yes, ma'am," Kema replies as she goes to her room to finish her homework.

After she finishes her homework, she gazes out the living room window like a cat waiting for its owner to return. Kema overhears Janice talking to Kema's grandmother, Granny Pauline, about Benjamin not being at home.

"Yes, Mama, I have called Gerald's house five times and left messages on the answering machine. I know you think Gerald is a bad influence on Ben; but he has been his best friend since they were kids. Ben promised me that he and Gerald had stopped going to the Player's Den since Gerald and Regina had their baby two years ago. Hold on, Mama, I have not told Kema to go to bed yet."

"Kema, it is past your bedtime, and you haven't had a bath. Sitting on the couch looking out the window will not make your father appear. I know you are worried about him, but he will be home."

Janice ushers Kema to the bathroom as she protests that she wants to wait for her father to come home. After her bath, Kema lays in bed but can't fall asleep. Her mind keeps racing with questions.

Did Daddy get hurt on his way home? Was he in the Player's Den with Gerald as I remembered Mama saying a while back doing who knows what with skanky women?

The following morning before Kema goes to school, Janice calls Benjamin's supervisor, Mr. Jones, at Vitality Trucking

Company and asks him if Benjamin had clocked out yesterday. Mr. Jones tells her that he was laid off a month ago.

"A month ago? Mr. Jones, are you sure you are not confusing Benjamin with another employee?"

"No, Mrs. Daniels I'm certain. We laid Ben off last month."

"Ok, thank you for letting me know."

As soon as Janice hangs up the phone, Kema looks at her and notices she has tears in her eyes.

"Mama, did you find out where Daddy is?"

"No, baby, but we will find him soon. It's time for you to catch the school bus and for me to go to work at the diner."

THREE

Benjamin has been missing since Wednesday night. Forty-eight hours have passed and now Janice knows that she could file a police report with the Chicago Police Department. She doesn't want to take Kema with her to the police station, so she plans to take her to Granny Pauline's house to stay for the weekend. When Kema arrives home from school on Friday, she notices an overnight bag sitting by the front door.

"Mama, are we going somewhere? Has Daddy come back?"

"I'm taking you to Granny Pauline's house to spend the weekend while I look for your Daddy."

"Why can't I stay with you while you look for Daddy?"

"Kema, I don't know if the places that I will go to look for your Daddy will be places kids can go. Besides, you will have more fun spending time with Granny Pauline. You always come back home happy asking me if a story Granny Pauline told you about me was true."

"Yes, but . . ."

"Don't worry, I will pick you up after church on Sunday afternoon."

Janice and Kema ride the bus to Granny Pauline's house. Kema always has a good time at Granny Pauline's, but this time is different. She wonders if Janice will pick her up as promised. Her Daddy hasn't come home yet and she doesn't want her Mama to disappear too.

As soon as Janice takes Kema to Granny Pauline's house, she catches a bus to take her to the police department. Once she enters the Eleventh District precinct, she goes to the front desk where an officer is seated.

"Yes, may I help you?"

"I would like to file a missing person's report for my husband, Benjamin Daniels."

"When was the last time you saw your husband, ma'am?" The officer inquires.

"I saw him on Wednesday morning before I *thought* he was heading to work."

"Do you think he was going to another place instead of work?"

"Who knows. I found out this morning that he was laid off from his job over a month ago."

"Have you tried to contact his family members or close friends to find out if they have seen or heard from him?"

"His parents died before I met him and although we have been married for ten years, I have never met his brother and sister. He told me that they live somewhere in the South. I called his best friend Gerald and left messages, but he has not returned my calls."

The officer shakes his head as if he has experienced this exact scenario many times. "Did you and your husband have an argument the night before?"

"We had an argument about him drinking too much, but it didn't get heated."

"Is there a bar or other place your husband likes to visit after work?"

"He used to go to this after-hours spot called the Player's Den with Gerald, but they stopped going two years ago."

"Have you tried going there to find out if anyone has seen him?"

"No, Officer, I haven't. He promised me that he had stopped going to the Player's Den."

"You should go to the Player's Den and ask if anyone there has seen your husband."

"That's a good idea, but I don't feel comfortable going there alone."

"I understand. Once I file the missing person paperwork, I can get one of my detectives to go to the Player's Den."

"When will he go?"

"In the next two to three weeks."

"What? Two or three weeks is too long to wait."

"Our department is overwhelmed with missing person cases and we simply don't have the manpower to get to your husband's any quicker than that."

"I guess I'll have to go myself and find out if anyone has seen him."

"Let us know if you find out anything."

"I will."

Although the Player's Den is located in a decent area in the Chicago's North Side, Janice is concerned about traveling alone back home to Burnside late at night. It will take her an hour to travel there by train and bus and another hour to return. She knows to walk quickly and be mindful of her surroundings. Janice is hoping that this will be her only trip to Player's Den as she approaches the broad-shouldered bouncer with a grimacing look who towers over her petite frame. She pulls out her wallet to show him a recent picture of Benjamin.

"Excuse me Sir, have you seen this man? His name is Benjamin Daniels—his friends call him Ben."

The bouncer looks at the picture for about three seconds and replies. "Lady, too many men come through this door. I can't recognize all of them."

Janice is not discouraged by the bouncer's response and continues. "He is my husband and he has been missing for two days. He used to frequent this club two years ago and I suspect that he has started coming here again since he was laid off from his job."

The bouncer does not attempt to hide his amusement before he responds. "I doubt someone broke would come to this club. There is a $40 minimum to spend on food and drinks, and he would have to have money to tip the dancers."

"I know he used to come here whenever he was stressed. Is there anyone else I can ask?"

"Yeah, you can ask Malik, the other bouncer. He'll be here tomorrow."

Janice did not plan to come back to this establishment, but if a return trip brings her closer to finding her husband, it will be worth it.

"Ok, thank you."

Although Janice hoped to find Ben in the Player's Den that night, she still remains hopeful that he will be found unharmed. Who would want to hurt Ben? He gets along with everyone and is a good judge of character. He promised Janice that he would give up gambling the last time he and Gerald came home drunk and broke two years ago after a night of shooting dice outside of the Player's Den. Janice told him that night that the next time he came home drunk and broke, he would no longer have a home with her.

FOUR

Benjamin and Janice

Janice always dreamed of having a girl that would have an enduring relationship with her father since she was not able to have a relationship with her own father. Janice's own father, William Monroe, died from a stroke a year after she was born. Janice only has one photo of him, in which he is holding Janice in his arms. He appears to be at least six feet tall and he is wearing a black suit, Fedora hat, and a broad smile. Janice relied on her mother, Pauline, to tell her about her father's character and his strong work ethic. William prioritized his family. When he learned Pauline was pregnant, he increased the coverage of his life insurance policy. Once he died, Pauline was able to use the life insurance settlement to purchase a home for her and Janice. During Janice's teenage years, Pauline encouraged her to find a good man to marry who could take care of her the way William had taken care of her.

When Janice met Benjamin, she was overwhelmed by his charm and good looks. He was six foot-three, with light brown eyes and a bronzy amber complexion that complimented the olive-green Army dress uniform he wore the first day she laid eyes on him. Benjamin had just been discharged from the Army when he walked into the diner where she worked as a waitress. Janice had seen a few men in uniform before, but none had captured her attention the way that Benjamin did. She would never forget the way he confidently walked in the diner as if he owned it. Benjamin sat down at the counter and made his order without looking at the menu. He maintained eye contact with her and smiled as he asked for black coffee, two slices of toast, three slices of bacon, and hard scrambled eggs. When Janice brought the food to him, she observed that he did not have a wedding band on his left ring finger or a mark that demonstrated that he had removed one prior to entering the diner. Benjamin smiled and thanked her for the food, and she returned his smile. As she was walking away, she felt that someone was watching her, so she looked back. She locked eyes with Benjamin, and he lifted his coffee mug as if he was giving her a toast and thanked her again. After Benjamin finished eating, Janice brought him his bill and he handed her a $20 bill and a note that said:

Janice,

Keep the change. Have the same order ready for me. I will see you tomorrow morning.

Benjamin

Janice's face felt flushed after reading the note. She tucked the note and the bill in her uniform pocket and smiled each time she ran her hand across her pocket that day.

Janice and Benjamin were inseparable after their initial meeting. Six months after they met, they were married. Pauline was not excited about Janice wanting to marry Benjamin without knowing his family's background or if he would be a good provider. Pauline wanted Janice to make sure there were not any "crazy" people in his family. Pauline believed that if Janice and Benjamin had kids, Benjamin could pass some of the "crazy" traits to their children. Janice assured her mother that if the children were crazy, she would keep them far away. Janice was certain that Benjamin would be a good provider since the day he wrote her that note. In addition, the week after they met,

Benjamin obtained a decent-paying job at Vitality Trucking Company unloading trucks. What Pauline wanted most was for Janice to be happy and although she was unsure of Benjamin, she saw how Janice glowed with contentment whenever she talked about him.

Janice was twenty years old and Benjamin was twenty-three when they were married at Chicago City Hall. Since Benjamin was only recently discharged from the Army, he had been renting a single room in a house. By Pauline's standards, this was not a suitable place for her daughter to stay. As a result, the newlyweds lived in the basement of Pauline's home on S Avenue on the South Side of Chicago. Benjamin didn't like the idea of living with Pauline because it made him feel emasculated. He agreed to move in only temporarily, until he could save up enough for a deposit on an apartment. Two months after Janice and Benjamin were married, Janice told Benjamin she was pregnant. Benjamin was excited about the pregnancy, but he knew that any money that he had saved to move out of Pauline's home would now need to be spent on the baby. Janice and Benjamin finally moved out of Pauline's home to their own apartment in Burnside when Kema was three. Only then did Benjamin feel that he was able to provide for his family.

FIVE

On Saturday, Janice makes the long journey back to the Player's Den. Just as the bouncer from the day before promised, another bouncer is at the door when Janice approaches.

"Excuse me, is your name Malik?"

"Yeah"

Janice pulls out her wallet and shows him Benjamin's picture. Malik looks at the picture for about 5 five seconds before saying, "That looks like Sweet Daddy."

Janice looks at Malik in disbelief before responding. "Sweet Daddy?"

"Yeah, I didn't know his name was Benjamin. He is in here now. I can take you to him."

Janice follows Malik into the Player's Den. It is smoky and dark, the only illumination coming from a glowing red light on the stage. The song "Nasty Girl" by Vanity 6 is playing in the background. As Janice follows Malik, she can't help but check out the stripper on stage who is dressed in a red lace teddy with matching garter straps and is gyrating on a stripper pole to the beat. Janice is feeling anxious and her heart is thumping so hard it feels as if it will burst out of her chest. Janice spots Benjamin at a table with his friend Gerald counting money.

"Benjamin, what are you doing in here? I have been worried half-crazy for the past two days trying to find you. I even contacted the police!"

"Janice, I can explain . . . remember when you told me not to come home if I was drunk and broke? Well, for the past two days I have been drunk and broke. I called Gerald to loan me some money, but he could only give me twenty bucks. Gerald said I would be better off using it on a dice game here for a chance to win more money. And, he was right! Just look at how much money me and Gerald won!"

"Yeah, how much of that money was given right back to the Player's Den? Why didn't you tell me you got laid off from VTC? I could have taken an extra shift at the diner and you could've stayed home with Kema until they called you back to work or you found another job."

"You know how I feel about not being able to provide for my family. I couldn't face you without having some money to give you to pay the bills."

"You are kidding me, right? You would rather have me and Kema worried to death about you than come home to talk about how we can fix our money problems. Unbelievable . . ."

"I think you all need time to talk," says Gerald as he gives Benjamin a smirk and quickly walks away from the table.

Before Benjamin can respond, the stripper who Janice saw on the stage dancing, saunters over.

"Hey, Sweet Daddy how bout you give me a few of those 20s you have in your hand. You know I am worth it . . ."

"Linda, it's not the time for this. This," he says motioning towards Janice, "is my wife Janice."

Linda examines Janice from head to toe and laughs. "You're Sweet Daddy's old lady? He told me he was shooting dice to get enough money to carry back to you." Linda places her hand on Benjamin's shoulder and moves it seductively down his chest before saying: "That's why he is not giving me my share of the cash."

Janice ignores Linda and continues addressing Benjamin. "How dare you Benjamin? After all these years of cooking, cleaning, and raising your daughter you would take up with this heifer."

"Heifer? I know you are not calling me a heifer. Your man wouldn't be here if he was gettin' what he needs at home."

Janice looks down to collect her thoughts and then raises both hands shoulder level as if surrendering. "It's fine, Benjamin. Now that I know that you are here at the Player's Den with Stripper Linda and your dice games, you don't need to worry about ever coming home. Kema and I will be just fine without you."

"Janice, you know I love you and Kema. I was trying to make things right."

"If disappearing, gambling, and spending time with a stripper is your way of showing love, Kema and I don't need it."

Janice rushes out of the Player's Den and takes the bus back to Burnside. On the bus, she thinks about all of Benjamin's broken promises to her. She also thinks about what she is going to tell Kema. Although Benjamin still lives, all the hopes, dreams, and promises she had about her family died once she saw him at the Player's Den.

SIX

Janice is restless after seeing Benjamin at the Player's Den. As soon as she returns home, she calls the precinct to let the officer handling the missing person case know that she found Benjamin at the Player's Den. She tosses and turns all night long thinking about breaking the news to Kema and Pauline. Janice resents that Pauline has been right about Benjamin. She realizes now that she should have heeded Pauline's advice and thought long and hard before saying "I do." Sunday arrives quickly for Janice and it is time to pick up Kema from Pauline's house. Hopefully, Pauline will comfort her instead of gloating that she was right. Janice says a prayer to herself before she knocks on Pauline's door. Pauline answers the door and sees Janice looking distraught.

"Hi, Mama. Where's Kema?"

"She's in the guest room playing. What's wrong? Did you find Benjamin?"

Janice's face reveals every emotion she wants to conceal. "Yes, I found him in the Player's Den with Gerald. While I was talking to Benjamin, some old stripper came over and acted like she and Benjamin were together! I told him never to return home and that Kema and I will be alright on our own."

"I know that you are upset, but he is still Kema's father and should be able to see her. You know how close they are."

Janice is surprised that Pauline seems to be taking Benjamin's side.

"Kema and I don't need the drama that he has caused. I will tell Kema about her father when we get home."

"I know how much you wanted Kema to have a good relationship with her father. Whatever is going on between you and Benjamin should not interfere with Benjamin and Kema's relationship."

"It seems to me that you are taking his side. . ."

"I'm not taking sides; I'm just standing on what is right. Kema needs her father in her life."

"I grew up without a father and I turned out fine. . ."

"By my prayers and the grace of God, you *did* turn out fine. But if Benjamin wants to be around his daughter, you should not stop him. I know he has his faults, but he loves Kema, and nothing can replace a father's love for his daughter. I bet the lack of a father's love is why there are so many women willing to strip for a living. The Player's Den will never need to look for employees because there are so many broken women looking for love in all the wrong places."

Janice looks at Pauline wearily and says, "Mama, I have heard enough." She loudly shouts, "Kema, gather your stuff so we can go home."

"You are upset right now. I understand. Just know that you and Kema will always have a place to stay here with me."

Kema gathers her belongings, kisses Granny Pauline, walks out the door, and heads with Janice to the bus stop. As soon as they board the bus and sit down, Kema starts to ask her mother questions about Benjamin.

"Is Daddy at home waiting for us?

"No, Kema. We will talk about your father when we get home."

"Did something bad happen to him?

"What did I say, Kema?"

Kema turns away from her mother and feels tears burning her eyes. She knows that whatever her mother is going to tell her will not be pleasant news. Although it is only a fifteen-minute bus ride from Granny Pauline's house to their apartment, it feels like three hours.

Before Janice can unlock the apartment door, Kema asks again about her father.

"Can we get inside the apartment?" Janice harshly responds.

"Yes, ma'am."

Kema does not want to experience more of her mother's temper and unpacks her clothes and takes her shower before joining her mother on the living room sofa.

Janice looks at Kema and says: "Kema, I found your father."

"Where is he now?"

Janice, takes a deep breath before responding. "He is in a place where troubled people go to escape their problems."

"Is he at church?"

"No, he is not at church."

"Is he in jail?"

"He is not in jail."

"Well, where is he? Why is he not coming home?"

"He is happier where he is."

"Did I make Daddy mad?

"You didn't make him mad."

"Is he mad at you?"

"Your Daddy is not happy with me."

"Can you make him happy so he will come back home?"

"I have done all that I can do to make him happy. When you get older you will understand that doing all you can do for someone is not always enough to keep the person happy."

Kema starts to cry. "Somebody is making Daddy happier than us that's why he is not coming home."

Janice pulls Kema close to her chest and hugs her tightly. "Kema, we will be alright. I love you and you know Granny Pauline loves you. You just need to focus on your schoolwork and make good grades. You know that if you continue to make good grades, you can get scholarships to attend college. Going to college and getting a good job will allow you to have many opportunities in your life so you won't be dependent on a man to help you financially."

Though Kema appreciates Janice's motivational talk, she is overwhelmed with sadness. *How could a few days of her Daddy being missing change her life?*

SEVEN

Janice takes extra shifts at the diner four days a week to help pay the bills. On the nights Janice works late, Kema rides the bus to Pauline's house after school and spends the night. Pauline thinks it would be easier if they move out of the Burnside apartment and move in with her. Janice doesn't see it that way. She has relied on Benjamin and her mother for too many things. Janice wants to demonstrate to Kema that hard work brings rewards. Her supervisor at the diner observes Janice's strong work ethic and promotes her to assistant manager within three months.

Kema's grades initially fall from all A's to all C's after her father leaves. However, she knows her mother is working hard to keep them afloat and doesn't want to disappoint her. Kema does what her mother told her to do: she put all her focus on making good grades. The following month, her grades return to straight A's. Kema maintains her high grades throughout the school year.

After Kema finishes her homework, she enjoys listening and dancing to music. Music and dance are her escape from the world. Her favorite genres are hip-hop, R&B, gospel, and pop. When Kema stays at Granny Pauline's house, she can only listen to Mahalia Jackson and Al Green without headphones. One day when Granny Pauline makes a quick trip to the store, Kema "forgot" the house rules and turns on Granny Pauline's stereo to play "Flava in Ya Ear" by Craig Mack. She has the music turned up so loud that she can't hear Granny Pauline come in the house.

"Kema, what are you listening to? Are you trying to wake the dead with this loud

noise?"

"I'm sorry, Granny."

"The way that you were bouncing your body to this noise, I didn't know if you were having a fit or a seizure."

"I was dancing."

"You call that dancing. . .step aside and let Granny show you how to dance."

Granny Pauline starts doing "The Twist" and the "Mashed Potato" to the beat of the song. Kema laughs and then dances along with Granny Pauline.

"I didn't know you liked to dance."

"I haven't been old my whole life, Kema."

Kema's love of dance and music helps her join the dance team in junior high and high school. Also in high school, she joins Junior Achievement, a program that encourages financial literacy and entrepreneurship, as well as the debate team, which strengthens her public speaking skills. During her senior year in high school, Kema is awarded a full scholarship to DePaul University.

Kema majors in Business Administration and stays on campus where she develops close friendships with the other students in her program. Although she maintains her strong work ethic, Kema allows herself to have fun with her friends. After long hours of studying during the week, they spend their weekends eating at the restaurants near campus. Occasionally, they sneak into a night club when they see the bouncer is not checking IDs. Once inside, they don't want to press their luck by ordering alcoholic drinks at the bar. They order soft drinks and sip them slowly as if they contain alcohol. Kema turns twenty-one during her senior year at DePaul and discovers that she likes all cocktails made with vodka. She remembers how her Daddy liked malt liquor. At this point, she doesn't want to drink anything that reminds her of her father.

She graduates Summa Cum Laude with a degree in Business Administration. Kema is heavily recruited by many companies, however it is Resilient Financial that catches her attention because of their focus on merging and acquisitions. Kema begins working there as a merger and acquisition analyst immediately after graduation and receives a promotion after her first year of employment. Resilient Financial invests in her career by providing her tuition assistance to pursue an MBA at the University of Chicago. She continues to work at Resilient Financial while pursuing a graduate degree. After two-and-a-half years, she earns an MBA—and another promotion.

Resilient Financial pays Kema well, which allows her to live in a three-bedroom condominium overlooking Lake Michigan in Chicago's Gold Coast. She tries to get Janice to move out of Granny Pauline's house—where she has lived since Pauline passed away a couple of months after Kema graduated from DePaul—and in with her, but Janice is satisfied where she is. Granny Pauline was not sick when she passed away, but died peacefully in her home. Kema thought God was keeping her around so she could observe Kema being an independent woman with a good job.

Granny Pauline would be proud of Kema. She has a great job, her own place, and pays her bills. Kema keeps a small circle of dependable friends. She confides mostly to her best friend, Sharon, who she met in high school. Sharon is a cosmetologist and owns two beauty salons in the city. Sharon is the only person Kema trusts with her hair, a key component of her professional appearance. Kema wears a flat-ironed bob with a part down the middle. To provide the finishing touches on her professional appearance, she has the nail technician at Sharon's salon give her a French manicure every two weeks.

From the outside, Kema has everything she needs and wants. The only thing missing from her life is male companionship. Kema has been so focused on completing her education and securing her financial future that she has neglected actively pursuing a partner. She has dated a few guys, but none have seemed to be interested in long-term relationships. Since Benjamin left, she has never really trusted men to follow through on their commitments. Maybe she had been receiving just what she expects from men: noncommitment. A few of her friends have suggested that she should talk to a therapist to sort through her abandonment issues. Kema would rather keep her mind off the past by staying focused on her goals. For Kema, that is therapy. Occasionally while lying in her bed, she wonders what happened to her father.

> *Is he homeless roaming the streets of Chicago?*
> *Did he lose his mind that day he didn't come home and forget he had a family?*
> *Did he start taking care of another family?*

Kema has always thought that Janice did not tell her the whole story of her father's disappearance. Kema tried questioning her again after she graduated from high school, but Janice's story remained the same: Benjamin left because he was happier someplace other than their home.

> *What was this place? If Kema found this place, would she find her father there?*

EIGHT

2019

"It's Ladies Night at the Player's Den. All ladies get in free before 11 p.m. Come to the longest running Ladies' Night in Chi-Town. The first 100 ladies to enter get a free cocktail courtesy of Sweet Daddy's Fashions."

Kema hears this announcement blaring from her car radio as she turns the final corner before she arrives home. *Why do they always think women are so thirsty for drinks and free admission? They need to advertise that all men that arrive to this Player's Den are single, have good jobs, and credit—then maybe I will think about going.* Kema's cellphone rings soon after she parks.

"Hello?"

"Kema what are you doing tonight?" Sharon asks.

"I'm going to eat some leftovers, take a bath, and go to sleep." Kema replies.

"Girl, you are so regimented. Let's check out Ladies Night at the Player's Den."

"Sharon, are you looking for an old player to play you?"

"No, I'm looking to step out and do something other than stay in the house. Girl, those leftovers will still be there when you get back."

"I didn't say that I was going," Kema replies playfully.

"Come on, Kema. I know you are not trying to find a player there, if anything we will get a free drink and a good laugh looking at all the old players."

"I could use a good laugh after a hard day. You know I'm working on a huge merger."

"Yes. I know. That is literally all you have been talking about lately. Look, if you don't have a good time, you can blame me, ok."

Kema laughs. "You know I will."

Sharon chuckles sarcastically and replies: "I will let that smart comment slide for now. The doors open at nine. I will meet you then."

"Ok, I'll see you at nine," Kema says.

Why did I agree to this? Kema thinks as soon as she hangs up the phone. *I don't have any clubbing outfits. I will have to wear my best 'straight-from-work-to-Happy-Hour' outfit.*

Kema arrives at the Player's Den at exactly 9 p.m. and sees a line of at least fifty women waiting by the entrance. Of course, Sharon is not among them. She knows whenever Sharon says that she will arrive at a certain time to add at least fifteen to twenty minutes to the promised time. Kema thinks to herself, *Who would have imagined that there would be a line for a Ladies Night at an old club? There must be a lot of thirsty women looking for a free drink.*

Sharon texts Kema at 9:16 p.m. to say she is walking towards the club. Kema sees Sharon a minute later and motions for her to get in front of her in the line.

"What's up with this line?" Kema asks Sharon. "You would think they were giving ladies free drinks and good men all night long."

"Well, since you are here, they might just do that."

"You've got jokes, Sharon."

"I have a few jokes stashed away," Sharon sarcastically replies.

A few minutes later the line moves and the ladies file into the Player's Den and receive numbered wristbands. The music inside the Player's Den is blaring as if trying to distract the ladies from thinking about how long they had to wait to get in. There is also a long line at the bar. Kema notices there are two bartenders making the promotional drink, a Cosmopolitan. There is also an older man in a three-piece black pinstriped suit with a red tie and matching handkerchief standing behind the bar. He smiles and greets every lady as he hands them their drinks. Kema thinks there is something familiar about his eyes and mannerisms; they remind her of her father. *Could this man possibly be her father? Not a chance*, she thinks. She hasn't seen her father in twenty-five years, he must be either dead or somewhere far away from Chicago. This older man looks like he has taken care of himself. Janice never did tell Kema the place where she last saw her father. Every time Kema asked, Janice replied only that it was a place where he had found happiness. Kema would be able to get a closer look soon because she and Sharon were next in line to receive their drinks.

"Hey Ladies, how are you doing tonight? Please accept your drinks courtesy of Sweet Daddy's Fashions. Enjoy yourselves tonight and remember to stop by Sweet Daddy's Fashion's and check out our men's and women's fashions before your next visit to the Player's Den."

"You sure are smooth, old dude. Are you Sweet Daddy?" Sharon asks.

"Yes, young lady, I am Sweet Daddy."

"It's good to see that you spend time among the people that patronize your store," Kema says.

"I have to see what people are wearing to make sure my inventory is up to date with the latest trends."

"Smart business, man. Thanks for the drinks, Sweet Daddy," replies Sharon.

"You're welcome, ladies."

Sharon and Kema leave the bar area with their Cosmopolitans and walk towards the dance floor.

"Sweet Daddy had it going on. I wonder if he has a Sweet Mama at home," says Sharon.

"Sharon, you *are* trying to find a sugar daddy in here!" Kema exclaims.

"Yes, if one approaches and is as smooth and good looking as Sweet Daddy, I'm willing to give him a chance."

"Girl, you need to stop," Kema admonishes her friend.

Beyoncé's song "Single Ladies" starts playing, and all the ladies rush to the dance floor, including Kema and Sharon. Kema is enjoying singing and dancing to the song but she can't help but think that she would have a better chance of relinquishing the "single lady" title if she visited a club with fewer single women and more single men.

After the song ends, the DJ makes an announcement over the PA, "We at the Player's Den would like to give a shout out to Sweet Daddy's Fashions for sponsoring tonight's Ladies Nights event. Let's all give a nice round of applause to Sweet Daddy aka Benjamin Daniels!"

Kema gasps and begins to feel nauseous. She turns to Sharon and asks: "Did the DJ say Sweet Daddy's name is Benjamin Daniels?"

"Yes, he said Sweet Daddy's name is Benjamin Daniels. Kema, you look like you have seen a ghost."

Kema grabs her lower abdomen and says, "Sharon, I have to get out of here. I'm not feeling very well."

"Ok, girl, we can leave."

Kema is visibly shaken as she and Sharon walk to her car.

"What's wrong Kema? Was the Cosmo too strong?" Sharon asks.

"No, it's not the drink. Do you remember me telling you that the last time I saw my father was when I was ten years old?"

"Yes, I remember. . ."

"My father's name is Benjamin Daniels."

"Kema, you can't be serious!"

"I'm serious. It's too late to go to my mother's place and tell her about this tonight."

"Could it just be a coincidence that Sweet Daddy has the same name as your father?" Sharon asks.

"It is possible, but I doubt it. I was looking at him before we approached the bar and I was thinking that he reminded me of my father."

"Are you going to be ok driving home?" asks Sharon.

"Yes, I'll be ok, though I may be up all-night thinking about this."

"Let me know when you get home."

"I'll call you as soon I get home," Kema replies.

Kema tries her best to concentrate at work the following day. She tossed and turned all night long thinking about how she would tell Janice that she thinks she saw her father. Kema calls Janice during her lunch break and tells her she will be stopping by to see her after work. The work day seems endless. As soon as 5 p.m. comes around, she walks briskly to her car and drives to Janice's house.

As soon as Kema opens the door, the aroma of baked chicken welcomes her. Kema does not have much of an appetite but knows that it will improve once she speaks to Janice about what happened last night.

"Hey, baby, can you wash your hands so we can eat?" Janice asks.

"Yes, mama. Before we eat, can I tell you what happened to me last night?"

"Sure, I'll keep the macaroni and cheese in the oven so it will stay warm."

Janice and Kema sit on the sofa in the living room. Kema takes a deep breath and begins telling her mother what happened.

"Sharon convinced me to go to the Player's Den with her last night for Ladies' Night. There was an older man handing out complimentary drinks at the bar. He reminded me of Daddy in his eyes and in the way he spoke to each lady as if she was the only one in the room. At some point, the DJ stopped the music and announced the complimentary drinks were provided by Benjamin Daniels, the owner of some place called Sweet Daddy's Fashions."

Janice looks as if she has seen the same ghost that Kema saw last night. She stares blankly at Kema.

"Mama, do you think that Daddy is still alive and has a store called Sweet Daddy's Fashions?"

Janice shakes her head in disbelief before responding. "Your father always loved flashy clothes . . ."

"Then it is possible that I could have seen Daddy last night?"

"I don't know how he got the money to start a clothing store . . . Maybe he hit the lottery after he disappeared. Where is this Sweet Daddy's Fashions located?"

"It must be close to the Player's Den because he was encouraging all the ladies to stop in his store before there next trip to the club."

"You said you saw him at the Player's Den? That place has been around since before you were born. It was a strip club back in the day."

"Once I find the location of Sweet Daddy's Fashions, will you go with me to see if this Benjamin Daniels is Daddy?"

"Kema, I think you should go by yourself. If you find that "Sweet Daddy" is your Daddy, you need to talk to him alone. If I see him, I may want to hurt him. I wouldn't want you to spend your hard-earned money to bail me out jail."

NINE

Kema returns home from dinner with Janice and searches online until she finds the address to Sweet Daddy's Fashions. She programs 613 Roosevelt Road into her Google Maps app to prepare for her journey. Kema thinks that she should call the store to see if Benjamin Daniels is there, however she doesn't want to lose her nerve or raise the suspicions of any employee who may answer the phone. If he is not there when she arrives, she will just look around the store. Kema sleeps well that night knowing that she has a plan in place to discover if Sweet Daddy is her father. She needs a good night's rest because the following day Kema has to present her final proposal on the acquisition of Unbelievable Foods to Mr. Flemings of Flemings International Foods.

Mr. Flemings is an eccentric character. You would think the owner of a multimillion-dollar company would come to a business meeting wearing business attire. Not Mr. Flemings. At every meeting with Kema, he has worn a brightly colored Hawaiian shirt, black shorts, and Birkenstock sandals. Looking at his meeting attire, you would assume that Mr. Flemings would not take the meetings seriously; however, he always arrives to their meetings fifteen minutes early. Kema doesn't want to keep Mr. Flemings waiting and meets with Mr. Flemings as soon as he arrives.

"Good afternoon, Mr. Flemings. How are you today?" Kema inquires.

"I'm doing well, Ms. Daniels. I'm looking forward to hearing your proposal."

"Yes, we have only a few weeks before the deal will close and I wanted to go over all the details with you."

Kema hands Mr. Flemings a copy of the proposal and he reviews the fifteen-page document and asks her questions. Kema believes most questions he asks are to verify that she has a thorough understanding of the deal. Kema was warned by her colleagues at Resilient Financial about Mr. Flemings' penchant for relentlessly quizzing anyone who works with him. It is his way of reinforcing his knowledge of the acquisition process and ensuring that anyone who represents him in a merger will be just as sharp—if not sharper—than he is. One hour had been allocated for the meeting, but with all of Mr. Flemings' questions it ran over by at least a half-an-hour. Kema has planned to leave work early to drive to Sweet Daddy's Fashions, so once she escorts Mr. Flemings from her office, she grabs her belongings, and swiftly walks out of the door.

Kema's heart is beating so hard she can feel her heartbeat through every inch of her body as she drives to Sweet Daddy's Fashions. She knows the questions that she wants to ask Benjamin Daniels, though, if it turns out that he is her father, she is scared he won't be happy to see her after twenty-five years. Does Kema want to inflict bodily harm on him like Janice said she does? Will she cry tears of joy or angry tears if he acknowledges that he is her father?

Kema parks across the street from the store and walks inside. She is greeted by a young man wearing a colorful hoodie and slim fit jeans.

"Welcome to Sweet Daddy's Fashions, my name is Darron. Can I help you find anything?"

"I'm looking for Benjamin Daniels. Is he in the store today?"

"Yes, he is in his office. Is there a problem with something that you recently purchased?" asks Darron.

"No, this is my first visit, but I would like to ask him some questions about the merchandise."

"Ok, I will see if he is available."

Darron goes to the back of the store and about two minutes later, Benjamin Daniels walks towards Kema displaying the same warm and welcoming smile she remembers from their brief interaction at the Player's Den.

He extends his hand for a shake and says, "Hello, I'm Benjamin Daniels. Darron told me you had some questions for me about the merchandise. Do you represent a clothing line that would like to sell your merchandise in my store?

"I don't represent a clothing line. My name is Kema, Kema Daniels. I spoke with you briefly at Ladies' Night at the Players Den two days ago." Kema replies.

Benjamin looks at her incredulously and takes a few steps back. "Did you say your name was Kema Daniels?"

"Yes, my name is Kema Daniels. My mother's name is Janice."

Tears emerge from Benjamin's eyes and he tilts his head towards the ground to wipe them away with the back of his hand.

"Kema, I have been trying so long to find you."

"Mama and I have never left Chicago. I don't know where you have been searching, but it shouldn't have been hard to find us. Mama said she found you at a place where you were happy and didn't want to leave . . . I still don't understand why you didn't come home. Did we make your life so miserable that you had to leave and create a new life?"

"Kema, its complicated. We need to sit down in a quiet place so I can explain everything to you. I never stopped loving you and wondering where you were and how you were living."

"You are right, your store is not the appropriate place to discuss personal matters. Can you meet me at Café Devour on E. 57th Street at eight?"

"Sure, I can meet you there at eight."

Kema exits the store and crosses the street to get to her car. She feels overwhelmed with emotions now that she has confirmed that the Benjamin Daniels, she saw at the Player's Den is her father. She sits in her car with her head on the steering wheel for about five minutes trying desperately to regain her composure. When she raises her head, she notices someone in a car sneering at her and waiting for her to leave the space. Kema starts her car quickly and drives home. Usually when she feels this anxious, she calls Janice to calm her down, but she knows that calling her mother now will only increase her anxiety.

TEN

Sweet Daddy's Backstory

Benjamin was certain that the relationship between him and Janice was over once she saw him at the Player's Den with Linda. She had endured Benjamin's drinking and gambling for a few years, but he knew her patience with him had a limit. Benjamin knew that Janice did not tolerate infidelity. The night Janice saw him and the Player's Den, he had not yet started a physical relationship with Linda Pérez, the stripper who had flirted with him in front of his wife. However, at the time Janice saw Benjamin at the Player's Den, he was guilty of having an emotional relationship with Linda. One night after gambling at the Player's Den, he told Linda that he felt defeated by being laid off from Vitality Trucking Company. He confided to her that he wanted to work to make sure that his family was financially stable. He was embarrassed for not living up to the expectations he set for himself and he felt he would only bring his family down by staying with them. Benjamin didn't want Kema growing up thinking that her father couldn't provide financially for his family.

After Benjamin finished telling her about his situation, Linda told him that he was a "Sweet Papi" for wanting to provide for his family. He was unsure what a "Papi" was, so Linda explained to him that "Papi" was a colloquial Puerto Rican expression of endearment that translated roughly as "Daddy." Benjamin liked the nickname "Sweet Daddy," so Linda called him that around the Player's Den. Before long, the regular customers and staff at the Player's Den were calling him "Sweet Daddy," too.

Linda told him that she wished that she had a man in her life who was serious about taking care of his obligations. After Benjamin left Janice and Kema, he slept on Gerald and Regina's couch. After a month of getting to know Benjamin, Linda asked him to move in with her. He agreed on the condition that all his money he won from gambling would be given to her to help with the rent. Though Linda enjoyed alcoholic beverages, she didn't drink nearly as much as Benjamin. Every time she saw him with malt liquor, she would gently remove the bottle from his hand and replace it with a Coke. Benjamin wouldn't protest when she did this because he knew it was her way of helping him.

Benjamin knew that gambling would not sustain him and decided to speak with Mr. Jones, his former supervisor at Vitality Trucking Company (VTC), to find out if the company planned on calling any workers back from the layoff. Mr. Jones said he would call Benjamin once the company was ready for workers to return. Two weeks after that conversation, Mr. Jones called him and said VTC had been awarded a five-year contract and needed freight unloaders in order to fulfill the contract. Benjamin begin working at VTC again, and, after receiving his first paycheck, decided to go to Janice's diner and give her some money to take care of Kema.

Janice was not happy to see him and told him that she and Kema didn't need him or his money. Benjamin tried again on three other occasions to leave money with Janice. Janice's supervisor, Mr. Carson, observed Benjamin's third attempt to give Janice money at the diner. When Janice had her back turned on her way to the kitchen to check on an order, he approached Benjamin and told him that he could leave the money with him and he would make sure Janice received the money as a bi-weekly bonus. He was sure that Janice would not become suspicious of the extra money because every day she gives 100% to her customers. In addition, Mr. Carson had planned on giving all the servers and the assistant manager additional money as an incentive for providing excellent customer service. Benjamin was not sure that he could trust the manager, but he was desperate to do something for his family. He believed that God would deal with Mr. Carson if he was not giving the money to Janice. Every other Friday before Benjamin started his shift at VTC, he would give Mr. Carson $200. To reassure Benjamin that he was giving the money to Janice, Mr. Carson would show him a copy of Janice's paystub which showed the additional $200 added to Janice's check.

After a year of working at VTC, Benjamin was promoted to Distribution Manager. He and Linda moved out of her apartment and rented a house on Chicago's Westside. Linda had stopped stripping at the Player's Den and was pursuing an Associate's Degree in Business Administration. Her goal was to go back to the Player's Den and manage the strippers after graduation. Benjamin was making enough money to support both of them so she didn't feel under any obligation to work and go to school. He enjoyed his position as a Distribution Manager and was able to purchase nice clothes and treat Linda to dinner at a fancy restaurant at least once a month. Although he enjoyed his job and found it rewarding, Benjamin had a desire to start his own business. Linda would joke with him that he could open up his own clothing store with all the suits he had. He thought that having a clothing store would serve two of his favorite activities: earning money and looking good. Benjamin opened up a savings account at the bank to put money away to eventually start his own business with. He took a second job as a salesman at a retail clothing store on the weekends in order to learn more about the business. He worked at VTC for eleven years before he felt ready to open his business—Sweet Daddy's Fashions.

Benjamin still worked at VTC for the first two years that Sweet Daddy's Fashions was open. Linda managed the store full-time and both she and Benjamin split duties when it came to hiring employees and ordering supplies. When Sweet Daddy's

Fashion became profitable in its third year, Benjamin decided to resign from VTC to work at Sweet Daddy's Fashions full-time.

The owner of a profitable small business, Benjamin finally felt ready to find Kema and let her know what he had made of himself. He knew several years had passed, and she likely would not want to see him. Janice had made it apparent that he was not welcome in their lives. He only knew that Janice and Kema had moved in with Granny Pauline after seeing the address on Janice's paystub during one of his exchanges with Mr. Carson. He knew Janice would consider it stalking should he show up to Granny Pauline's home uninvited to see Kema. He had too much to lose now and didn't want to do anything that could jeopardize his new life. Much as he hated being away from his daughter, he knew Janice was a strong woman who could take care of Kema.

Janice had never filed for divorce from Benjamin, and Linda never pushed Benjamin to divorce Janice and marry her. She was content with their life together and didn't need a piece of paper from the government to prove that Benjamin loved her. Linda had seen far too many of her friends who had lived with their partner for ten years or more finally decide to get married only to end up getting a divorce within two years. Linda was not going to let that be her fate. She and Benjamin were business partners and both of their names were on the lease to the house they were renting. Linda was secure that she would be taken care of if something were ever to happen to Benjamin.

With Linda's encouragement, Benjamin reduced his drinking to only on special occasions, though he was far from the picture of health. He drank a can of Coke with every meal and didn't believe a meal was complete without meat. The only green thing Linda could get him to eat was the green beans she prepared for dinner every Sunday. Despite his diet, he remained slim. He did have a couple of heart attacks due to his poor diet and the stress of running a small business. These heart attacks only slowed him down for a month at a time. While he recuperated, Benjamin knew he could rely on Linda to take over his responsibilities at Sweet Daddy's Fashions and he had acquired a reliable staff.

Though Benjamin did not attend church, he would occasionally pray to God that he would see his daughter again so that he could let her know that, though he hadn't been there for her, he had never stopped loving her. It appeared that God had finally answered his prayers.

ELEVEN

Confrontation

Kema arrives at Café Devour at 7:46 p.m. for her 8 o'clock meeting with her father. She arrives early to find a table in the rear of the establishment where she can observe Benjamin as he walks in and looked around for her. Will he look around the Café anxiously for her thinking that she has stood him up? Will he think the meeting is a set up for a confrontation? Will he come in wearing a large smile as confident as the one he had at the Player's Den? Kema orders a cup of chamomile tea as she waits for Benjamin to arrive.

Benjamin walks in the café at exactly eight o'clock and Kema's initial thoughts are correct: he looks as if had just run away from someone chasing him down the street. He pulls out a handkerchief to wipe his brow and looks around the café for Kema. Benjamin sees her raised hand and walks to the rear table where she is seated.

"I see that you made on time," Kema says.

"Yes, I couldn't miss catching up with my baby girl," Benjamin replies.

"I don't know if I can be called your baby girl because it has been at least twenty-five years since I last saw you," Kema remarks snidely.

Benjamin looks at her nervously. "True. You have grown up to be just as pretty as Janice," Benjamin observes. "How is your Mama?"

"She is fine. She retired from the diner two years ago," Kema replies.

"I'm glad to hear that she is doing good. I have to admit that I was scared to meet up with you. I was thinking Janice would be with you along with the cast and crew of Iyanla Vanzant's show 'Fix My Life,'" Benjamin says and laughs nervously.

Kema is not amused with his attempt at humor and responds, "I don't think that show is ready for all of our baggage."

"I see you like to joke around just like me," Benjamin says.

"Our situation is not a joke. Do you know that I cried every night for about a month after you left?" Kema angrily responds.

Benjamin breaks eye contact and looks down at the table. "I can't imagine how you felt. I know saying 'I'm sorry' is not going to take away all the hurt and pain. I was a troubled man back then and didn't know how to handle being a husband and a father. I needed time . . ."

"Time! Time for what? How much time did you need? Did you ever think about me or try to find me? All these years have passed, and I never knew the reason you abandoned us. Every time I asked Mama, she would tell me you found a place that made you happier than being with us."

"Kema, I was addicted to gambling and alcohol back then. I needed time to get myself together and show you that I had become a better man. Your Mama gave me plenty of chances to get it together, but I knew the last time I messed up that I could not come back."

"I was ten when you left. I wasn't worried about how much you drank or gambled. All I knew was that my father was gone, and I couldn't help but think it was my fault. I haven't had a serious relationship with a man because I fear if I let one get too close, then he will leave me."

"I don't blame you for not having a relationship because these men out there today are no good."

"I needed your advice on men when I was young—I don't need it now."

Benjamin dejectedly looks up at Kema. "Just know that I'm here now to give you advice . . . or anything else you need."

Kema raises her right hand towards Benjamin to put a stop to their conversation. "This is becoming too much for me right now. I need to leave," Kema replies.

Benjamin pulls out a business card from his jacket pocket and writes his cell phone number on the back. "If you want to talk again, my cell number is on the back of this card. Call me anytime."

Kema reluctantly takes the card and places it in her purse as she rushes out of the café.

TWELVE

Speaking with her father brought out all the hurt she has repressed over the years. She knows she won't be able to sleep well if she doesn't drive to Janice's house tonight to tell her about the meeting. Kema calls Janice and tells her that she is on her way. Once Kema pulls up to her mother's house, her anxiety starts to diminish. Kema thinks that now that she has spoken to her father that Janice will tell her why she never revealed where she saw him.

"Did your father show up to the café?" Janice asks.

"Yes, and he gave me a lame excuse on why never tried to contact me all these years," Kema replies.

"I didn't think it was a good idea to meet with your father. Why would you resurrect the dead?" said Janice.

"Mama, can you now tell me where you saw Daddy?" Kema asks.

Janice sighs deeply, rubs her right hand over her left hand before she replies, "I saw him in the Player's Den."

Kema looks confused. "You are telling me I saw Daddy at the same place that you saw him?"

"Yes, I guess your Daddy still enjoys the Player's Den. You would think he would have found somewhere else to gamble and drink."

Kema shakes her head in disbelief. "Why didn't you tell me this years ago?" I can understand not telling me as a kid, but I asked you when I turned eighteen, when I was an adult."

"I didn't want you to get distracted from your responsibilities. You know if I told you then you would have tried to find him to confront him. We didn't have the time to worry about your Daddy. Making sure you received an education and a good job were our priorities."

"Mama, you didn't give me the option to decide for myself. You just assumed that I couldn't handle knowing that my father was still in Chicago."

"Listen Kema, I did my best raising you to become the independent woman that you are today. Maybe I should have told you, but you know what they say: hindsight is 20/20." Janice replies.

"I just don't know what to think anymore . . . I need time to process all of this . . . I'll talk to you later, Mama."

"Now, Kema don't just go off and pout . . . Please call me when you get home?"

"Sure . . ." Kema replies as she walks towards the door.

Kema gets in her car to drive home. Thoughts are running around her mind as if in a marathon. Although Janice finally revealed where she saw her father, it did not bring Kema any peace or sense of closure. Benjamin certainly seemed open to seeing her again. However, Kema feels she needs to complete the Flemings International Foods and Unbelievable Foods merger before she attempts any reconciliation with him. Maybe Janice was right. Her focus has allowed her to accomplish many goals. Kema is close to reaching a career milestone that few her age has achieved. She can't let her estranged father sabotage her chance of becoming Managing Director of Mergers and Acquisitions at Resilient Financial.

THIRTEEN

At work the next day Kema can't stop thinking about her father. She has so many questions to ask him. The top two questions are:

Does she have any siblings?
Do her drive and ambition come from him?

Kema decides that she should see Benjamin again to get her questions answered. She digs in her purse and pulls out the business card he gave her. Kema studies the business card like she is preparing to take an exam. After staring at the card for ten minutes, Kema takes out her cell phone and dials Benjamin's number. The call goes to voicemail after the first ring and Kema does not leave a message. Two minutes later, Benjamin calls her back.

"Hello, this is Kema."

"Kema, I'm glad that you called. How are you doing?" Benjamin asks.

She is annoyed by his question and wants to respond by saying, *How the hell do you think I'm doing?* but she choices civility and simply answers, "I'm doing ok. I just called to ask if we can continue our discussion."

"I would love that, Kema. Would you like to come over for dinner tomorrow night around seven?" Benjamin asks.

"Sure, what is your address?

"My address is 234 W. 35 Street," Benjamin replies.

"Should I bring anything?" Kema inquires.

"No, all you have to do is bring your appetite." Benjamin cheerfully replies.

"Ok, then. I'll see you tomorrow at seven."

Kema has no memories of her father cooking. Janice always cooked their meals. *Had he learned to cook over the years or was he going to order food for them?* Kema snaps back from her thoughts. She should not be thinking about the dinner menu right now, she should be more concerned about the questions she wants to get answers to during the dinner.

Kema leaves work the following day at six to drive to Benjamin's house. She knows if she stops off at home first, she will second guess her decision to go. Kema made a commitment to have dinner with her father and her sense of responsibility will not allow her to renege. She knows her conscience will not leave her alone if she does come up with an excuse not to go to Benjamin's for dinner. That doesn't mean she won't feel a sense of relief if *he* decides to cancel.

Kema pulls up to Benjamin's house which is a brick bungalow with a small fenced-in front yard with two manicured bushes under the left window. Kema walks to the door, takes a deep breath, and rings the doorbell. After around twenty seconds, the door opens slowly and she is greeted by a petite Hispanic woman with salt and pepper hair pulled up in a bun.

"You must be Kema. I'm Linda. Come in. Your father is in the bathroom cleaning up right now."

As Kema walks inside the smell of stewed beef, onions, and peppers tantalizes her nostrils. As Kema is still pondering who Linda is to Benjamin, Benjamin enters the living room and greets her.

"Kema, welcome to our home. I hope you are hungry. Linda has been slaving in the kitchen all day to make ropa vieja, arroz con gandules, and tres leches cake."

Kema thinks, *Our home? He did not say he had a wife . . . I don't think he ever divorced Mama . . . When did he learn Spanish?"*

"I had to make a special meal to honor your first visit." I have heard so much about you over the years and it is such a pleasure to finally meet you," Linda says.

"Thank you Mrs . . ." Kema attempts to respond but is cut off by Linda.

"My last name is Pérez. But you can call me Linda."

"Thank you, Linda," Kema responds. Kema thinks, *Ok, maybe he is not a polygamist after all.*

Linda ushers Kema and Benjamin to the dining room table and serves them food.

"Kema, Benjamin did not tell me if you had any dietary restrictions. I hope you do not have any food allergies or are a vegetarian. He just told me that you were coming to dinner and that I should prepare a good meal. Men never give as many details as we would like."

"I have no food allergies or dietary restrictions," Kema replies.

"Great, then I hope you will enjoy the meal," says Linda.

Kema takes a few bites of the ropa vieja and arroz con gandules and both are delicious. It is certainly nothing like her mother's cooking, but after tasting Linda's food, she can understand why Benjamin has been in a long-term relationship with her. While she may not have any memories of her father actually cooking, she does remember that he always enjoyed a good meal. Kema thinks to herself, *what else does she have to offer besides her domestic skills?*

"How long have you known my father?" Kema asks.

"I have known your father for around twenty-five years. We met while I was a dancer at the Player's Den," Linda replies casually.

"Are you telling me you have known my father ever since he left me and my mother?" Kema asks incredulously.

Linda looks at Benjamin as if seeking permission to answer Kema's question. Benjamin subtly nods his head and Linda answers the question.

"Yes, we were friends first. I saw him at the Player's Den several times counting his money after winning dice games.

One day I asked him who was he playing those games for and he told me that he had lost his job and had promised his wife that he would not gamble again. He said he couldn't go home to face his wife and daughter, that he would rather let her think that something had happened to him than disappoint her again. I encouraged him to return home and explain the situation to your mother," Linda explains. "I don't know if you were old enough to know how stubborn your father can be. Once he has his mind set on doing something a certain way, it is hard to convince him to change."

"Mama always told me that my stubbornness came from my father."

"I'm also glad that you came to dinner tonight," says Linda, "because if you didn't, Benjamin would have asked me to make fried chicken. The doctor has warned him to stop eating it to prevent him from having another heart attack."

"You seem to take really good care of my father. Do you have any children?"

"I don't have any children. Taking care of your father, my nieces and nephews, and looking out for the team at Sweet Daddy's Fashions has satisfied my desire to have any children," Linda replies.

Kema takes in all this information as she moves her food around her plate. Benjamin observes that Kema still has a habit of playing with her food when she is thinking.

"Baby girl, what else would you like to ask?" Benjamin inquires.

"Do *you* have any kids?" Kema asks Benjamin.

Benjamin turns to Linda, smiles, grabs Linda's right hand and kisses it. "No, I have been with Linda and no one else for the past twenty-five years. She encouraged and helped me to establish Sweet Daddy's Fashions." Benjamin looks across the dining room table at Kema and adds, "I have been praying for the day when I could show you the store. Who would have thought that we would be reunited in my store? God works in mysterious ways."

Kema does not say anything. She looks at her father and his girlfriend and smiles then studies her plate as she tries to think of an excuse to leave early. She has asked the questions she wanted to ask, now she wants time to herself to consider the answers. Kema turns her attention away from the plate and opens her purse to take out her cellphone. She glances at the time and remembers that she has a meeting with Mr. Flemings in the morning.

"Thank you for dinner, Linda. Unfortunately, I need to leave now because I have an early meeting with a client tomorrow morning," says Kema apologetically.

"You are welcome in our home anytime, Kema, and you can stop by Sweet Daddy's Fashions if you have time during the day," replies Linda.

"Yes, I would love for you to see what we are doing at Sweet Daddy's Fashions," echoed Benjamin.

FOURTEEN

When Kema arrives at the office the next day, she is distracted by her thoughts of the previous evening. She wonders how different her life—and his life—would have been if Benjamin had stayed with her and her mother. Would he have been inspired to start a business? Would he have struggled to retain employment throughout her childhood? She heard that children raised in single-parent homes often strive harder to achieve their goals than children raised in two-parent homes. Maybe it was her destiny for her father to leave when she was a child and then return when she is older. In the middle of her thoughts, Marsha, Kema's administrative assistant, informs her that Mr. Flemings has arrived.

Kema tells Marsha to send him in. Kema greets Mr. Flemings with a smile and a handshake before they both take their seats. Kema notices that Mr. Flemings is studying her face. She knows that he can be a bit eccentric, but today feels different. She is made uncomfortable by his because it feels like he is trying to see her innermost thoughts.

"Is something wrong, Mr. Flemings?" Kema inquires.

"I was about to ask you the same question, Ms. Daniels. Are *you* ok?"

"Yes, I am fine. Thank you for your concern," says Kema flatly, trying to keep the meeting on track.

"I'm not so sure that you are. In our previous meetings, you had more energy and your handshake was a bit firmer," says Mr. Flemings.

"I'm just a little tired this morning, that's all," Kema replies.

Mr. Flemings seems determined to find out what is wrong with Kema. "Are you stressed about the upcoming meeting? You have nothing to fear. Under your leadership, I'm confident that the meeting will run smoothly. If it isn't the merger meeting that is worrying you, then what could it be? Why don't you just open up a bit and share what is troubling you?"

Kema takes a deep breath and decides to tell Mr. Flemings the truth. Before she knows it, she begins to tell Mr. Flemings about how she recently reunited with her estranged father after twenty-five years. In addition, she tells him that she resents her father wanting to reconnect with her and show her his business and she shares her frustration that this is all during the biggest merger deal of her young career.

Mr. Flemings pauses, looks solemnly at Kema, and then tells her how he wishes he had the opportunity to reconnect with his son, Jake. He relates to her that after he and his wife divorced, she and seven-year-old Jake moved to Nebraska to be closer to her family. Mr. Flemings says he has dedicated his life establishing Flemings International Foods with the goal of passing the business on to Jake. Although he didn't visit Jake in Nebraska and didn't spend much time with him when he came to Chicago during his summer breaks, Mr. Flemings says that he thought his son would grow up to understand that he was working hard to allow him to be financially secure.

Unfortunately, Mr. Flemings was unable to explain this to Jake because he was killed in a car accident on a two-lane highway in Nebraska soon after his high school graduation.

Mr. Flemings looks as if he is fighting back tears that are eager to burst from his eyes. He looks at Kema and says, "I regret not spending all the time that I could have with my son. After his death, I realized how fragile life can be. After Jake died, I got involved with a spiritual community here in Chicago where I have been learning to appreciate every moment I have on this earth. We are here today in this moment, but in the next breath, we could be gone from this earth. I think you should get to know your father again while you have time."

Kema is deeply moved by Mr. Flemings display of vulnerability. "I'm sorry to hear that you lost your son. Thank you for sharing your wisdom with me."

"You're welcome, Ms. Daniels. Now that the negative energy has been cleared from this space, I think we are ready to start our meeting."

FIFTEEN

As Kema is driving home from work, she thinks about Mr. Flemings and his son. She thinks that maybe all that she had considered eccentric in his behavior could be the result of the pain he has experienced from losing his son. She also thinks about how she really needs to work on her "poker face" and body language to prevent additional prying from Mr. Flemings or any of her work colleagues. Although she has always been skeptical of sharing her personal life with people from work and clients, Kema feels a burden has been lifted from her after sharing her concerns with Mr. Flemings. Instead of going home, she decides to visit Sweet Daddy's Fashions.

Kema enters Sweet Daddy's Fashions and is again greeted by Darron, the young man she saw on her first visit.

"Welcome to Sweet Daddy's Fashions! My name is Darron. Can I help you find something this evening?"

"Hello, Darron. My name is Kema, I believe I met you the last time I was here and asked to speak with my father, Benjamin Daniels," says Kema.

Darron looks confused and then asks, "You are Mr. Daniels' daughter?"

"Yes, I am. And I would like to ask you a few questions as you help me pick out a nice outfit."

"Ok . . ." Darron replies somewhat awkwardly. "Are you looking for something casual or something to wear out at night?

"I'm looking for a casual outfit that I can also wear on the weekends," Kema responds.

Darron guides her to the casual section.

"How long have you worked at Sweet Daddy's Fashions?"

"I've worked here for almost two years now. Mr. Daniels saw me hanging outside the store with two of my friends after closing the store one night. He told us that he had a job for us to do if we would meet him at the store at 7:00 am that Saturday morning. My friends were not interested in getting up that early and thought that I was crazy for wanting to do it, but I wanted to make some extra money to help my Mom. I told my Mom about Mr. Daniels and his offer and she came with me to Sweet Daddy's Fashions that Saturday to meet him and to make sure his offer was legit. I sorted and folded the clothing on that first day for three hours and he paid me $50! After the first Saturday working for him, he told me that I could sort and fold clothes every Saturday during the school year and he would increase my hours and duties during the summer."

"Do you enjoy working here?"

"I like working here. Mr. Daniels is fair and has given me good advice about school and life. School and work take up most of my time so I don't have time to hangout on the corner anymore. My Mom is glad because she didn't like me hanging outside at night with my friends. One of my old friends is in juvenile detention now for armed robbery. That could have been me. Because Mr. Daniels has taken the time to show me how the business works, I plan to study Business Administration when I go to college next fall."

"That's very impressive, Darron," responds Kema before she turns her attention to a navy blue and white French terry jogging suit. She picks up the suit and tells Darron, "This is exactly what I'm looking for. Thank you so much for your help."

"You are welcome. A new pair of shoes will go well with your new jogging suit. Would you like to see what kinds athletic footwear we have in stock?" asks Darron.

"Yes, let me see what you have available."

Darron leads Kema over to the athletic footwear and she decides to purchase three pairs of low-cut white socks and white shell toe tennis shoes along with her jogging suit.

"Darron, please escort me to the cash register before I decide to buy anything else!"

"Yes, Ma'am. Do you want me to get Mr. Daniels for you?"

"No, I don't want to disturb him. I'll catch up with him another day."

While Kema is driving home from Sweet Daddy's Fashions, she is feeling torn. She is glad to know that Benjamin has made such a positive impact in Darron's life. However, she secretly wishes that he had been around to guide her life decisions. As she is turning onto her street, her phone rings.

"Hello?"

"Kema, this is Linda. Your father was just rushed to the hospital."

"Wait? What? What happened?"

"He was working at his desk in the store and he called out that he was having chest pains. Darron called 911 and then called me. He's had another heart attack."

"Ok . . . What hospital is he at?"

"Gorreta."

"I'll be there as soon as I can."

Kema hangs up the phone and takes a deep breath. The last thing that Mr. Flemings said keeps replaying in Kema's mind, *I think you should get to know your father again while you still have time.*

Kema looks in both directions to ensure no car is coming and performs a U-turn in the middle of the street. She presses hard on the accelerator and speeds to Gorreta Hospital. Kema doesn't know what to expect when she arrives.

SIXTEEN

"I'm looking for Benjamin Daniels." Kema informs the receptionist when she arrives at the hospital. "Do you know what room he is in?"

"What is your relation to Mr. Daniels?" replies the medical receptionist.

"I am his daughter, Kema Daniels."

Linda hears the conversation between Kema and the medical receptionist and darts over to greet Kema.

"Kema, I'm glad you made it."

"How is he?"

Linda saunters back to the waiting area and takes a seat. Kema follows her. "He is in ICU. If he improves in the next twenty-four hours, he will be moved to recovery in a regular room and monitored by doctors," replies Linda.

"How are you doing?" Kema asks.

"I could be better. This is your father's third heart attack, and it scares me each time. I have tried to get him to eat better and to not work so much, but your father is one stubborn man."

"It's so strange, I stopped by Sweet Daddy's Fashions today on my way home from work. I even purchased a few items from Darron, who seems to be an intelligent and hardworking young man."

Linda looks at Kema skeptically then asks, "Did you talk to your father while you were there?"

"No, I didn't want to disturb him."

Linda wearily nods her head, looks down at the floor, and says, "Ok, I know you were not expecting to spend your evening worried about your father. You can go home if you want. I can always call you once I get any updates on his condition."

"Have you had anything to eat?" Kema asks.

"No, I was preparing dinner when Darron called. To tell you the truth, I'm not feeling hungry."

"I can get you something now from the cafeteria and you can eat it later." Kema offers.

Linda nods her agreement and Kema asks the receptionist for directions to the cafeteria. Once there, she purchases a turkey sandwich and a ginger ale for Linda.

Kema walks back to the waiting area where she finds Linda standing up and watching CNN on the television screen.

"Linda, I got you a sandwich and ginger ale. I hope you like turkey."

Linda slowly turns away from the television and towards Kema and says "Thank you. I appreciate you doing this for me. How much do I owe you?"

"Don't worry about paying me back. Do you plan to stay here all night? Do you need me to go to your house to get you anything?"

"My sister Camila is coming with a change of clothes. She said she'll stay and sit with me tonight."

"I'm glad to know you won't be alone."

"No, I will not be alone. Thank you, Kema, I will call you in the morning or if there is any news."

Kema gathers her purse and walks to the parking lot. It is almost nine and it is only now that she realizes *she* has not had anything to eat. She opens the car door, slumps into the seat, locks the door, and looks at her phone. There are two missed calls and a voicemail from her mother.

It has been two days since Kema last spoke with Janice. They usually do not go more than one day without speaking. Kema knows her mother is worried about her and that she needs to check in with her to alleviate her fears. She decides that she will return her mother's call once she has eaten a small bowl of pineapple and is relaxing on her couch listening to Jill Scott with a hot cup of chamomile tea.

But before she can pour her tea, her mother calls.

"Hello, Mama."

"Kema, I have been trying to get in touch with you. I hope you haven't been avoiding me because of our conversation a couple of days ago."

"I'm sorry, Mama. I have been busy with work and tonight Daddy had a heart attack and was taken to the hospital."

"Who told you? I thought you only met him that one time at the café. I didn't think you would contact him again."

"Linda, Daddy's girlfriend, called and told me."

"Linda? Is that the same heifer who your Daddy left me for? How did she get your number?"

"I didn't give her my number. I guess Daddy gave it to her in case of an emergency.

I thought about what you said about not contacting Daddy, but during my meeting with Mr. Flemings today, I told him about my situation with Daddy and he encouraged me to reconnect with him."

"Mr. Flemings? Is that the guy who you are working with on the merger? Why would you tell him about your personal life? Bringing your personal life to the office is not going to help you climb the corporate ladder."

"I didn't mean to tell him. He could just sense something was bothering me and he wouldn't let up until I told him what it was."

"You could have told him you weren't feeling well or something else other than your personal business. The last thing you need is someone using your personal life against you in a tough negotiation."

Kema rolls her eyes and is thinking that she does not need this lecture from her mother about how to conduct her business affairs. As calmly as she can, Kema replies, "I appreciate your concern, Mama. I don't think Mr. Flemings would use my conversation with him against me."

"Ok, I guess you know better than I do, though I would certainly not make it a habit to reveal personal information to your business associates."

Kema decides that the conversation is getting too intense and deftly changes the subject, "Enough about me, how are you doing?"

"I'm doing alright. I have a doctor's appointment next Thursday afternoon. I wanted to ask if you could pick me up on your way home from work, but now that you are so busy with your father, I don't know if you will have time to do it."

Kema is doing all she can to keep the annoyance from her voice when she responds, "Mama, you know I always make time for you. You have supported me my entire life. I'm just getting to know Daddy right now. It's past your bedtime, Mama, and I know you get a little cranky when you are sleepy. I love you and I will call you tomorrow."

"Ok, baby. I love you too."

Kema arrives at work the next morning thinking that Linda will likely call her soon with an update about her father. As she is returning from her lunch break, she receives the expected call.

"Hello?"

"Hi, Kema. I just wanted to let you know that your father's condition has stabilized and he has been moved from the ICU. His doctor said he should be well enough to receive visitors this evening. I'm sure he would be happy to see you."

"I will visit him after work. Are you still at the hospital?"

"No. Camila just brought me home and is making sure I rest before I return to the hospital tomorrow."

"Thank you for the update."

"You're welcome."

SEVENTEEN

Kema leaves work at five and drives to Gorreta Hospital. She checks in with the receptionist and a nurse is called to escort her to Benjamin's room. The nurse gently opens the door and Kema sees Benjamin is sleeping.

"Did I come at a bad time?" Kema asks.

"Not at all. Your father has been sleeping on and off throughout the day." The nurse gently taps Benjamin's left shoulder. "Mr. Daniels . . . Mr. Daniels . . . you have a visitor."

Benjamin slowly opens his eyes, blinks, and smiles when he sees Kema. "Baby girl, you came to see me."

"Hi, Daddy. I am sorry that I have to be seeing you under these circumstances. Linda told me that you have been working long hours. You may want to slow down and take care of yourself a little better."

"I know, I know. But I got a late start on my life, and there is still so much that I want to do. Maybe I can slow down a bit now that you are back in my life and I know that my legacy is in good hands."

Kema thinks: *Legacy? One neighborhood clothing does not make a legacy. Keep your emotions in check, don't let your face tell him what you are thinking.*

"I stopped by Sweet Daddy's Fashions yesterday and spent some time with Darron. He seems like a sharp young man who is more than capable of taking care of the store in your absence.

I think the store will be in good hands if you take time off to recover."

"I knew Darron was sharp the first time I saw him hanging outside of my store a couple of years ago with those knuckleheads that he called friends. Something about the look in his eyes reminded me of myself when I was his age. My conscience wouldn't allow me to ignore him and not offer to help him."

Now he has a conscience? Where was his conscience when he left our family? Kema allows this thought to pass before she responds. "It looks like you have been a good mentor to him as well. He told me he will be going to college in the fall to study business administration."

"Yeah, I'm really proud of Darron."

The nurse abruptly enters the room and announces: "I'm sorry, but I am afraid that visiting hours are over; it is time for Mr. Daniels to rest for the evening."

After the nurse's announcement, Benjamin's facial expression changes and he looks weaker than when Kema first entered his room.

"Good night. The next time I see you, I hope you will be out of the hospital," Kema says.

Benjamin gives a slight nod to Kema and she leaves the room.

After a two-day stay in the hospital, Benjamin is discharged on Saturday morning. Linda calls Kema to let her know that he is home and Kema lets Linda know that she plans to visit in the afternoon. When Kema arrives, Linda answers the door looking as if she has not slept in a week. She smiles at Kema and leads her to the master bedroom where Benjamin is fast asleep.

Linda places her hand on Benjamin's shoulder and whispers, "Ben, Kema is here."

Benjamin slowly opens his eyes and a wide smile appears on his face as if has just won the lottery.

"Baby girl, good to see you."

Linda smiles, turns to Kema, and says, "I'll leave so you two can talk."

"Don't go too far now, I may need a nurse," Benjamin responds flirtatiously.

Linda turns to him and winks. "I'll be in the kitchen if you need me."

Kema feels a tinge of resentment towards her father. The flirting between Linda and Benjamin reminds Kema of how Janice and Benjamin used to flirt when she was a child. She tries to shake the memory from her mind and smiles at Benjamin.

"How are you feeling today?"

"Not too bad for an old man. The doctor says I have to eat rabbit food for the rest of my life and exercise to prevent another heart attack."

"Are you going to take the doctor's advice?"

"I will eat a banana in the morning with my bacon and egg biscuit. But I hate the taste of raw vegetables. I read too many stories about produce being recalled for having bacteria and making people sick. If food is going to take me out, I want to enjoy it first."

"The banana sounds like a good start, but I think you should reconsider the bacon and egg biscuit."

"I don't know about that, Kema. I'm that dog from the old Beggin' Strips commercial that keeps saying, 'Bacon, Bacon, Bacon! I love Bacon!'"

Kema laughs at her father's devotion to bacon and responds, "I see you are passionate about your food."

Benjamin smiles and reaches for Kema's hand. "Grab the chair from Linda's vanity and have a seat beside me."

Kema goes to the other side of the room and carries the chair over to the side of the bed.

Benjamin looks lovingly at Kema and says, "You haven't told me anything about your life. I don't even know what you do to earn a living. I know it is something important because I saw you drive away in a silver Porsche 911 after you had dinner with us."

"I'm the Director of Mergers and Acquisitions at Resilient Financial."

"Resilient Financial? You are a director at the largest bank in Chicago!"

"I am hoping to be promoted to Managing Director once I close a big deal next Thursday."

"That's my Baby Girl! What company is the client from?"

"I signed an NDA. I'm not allowed to talk about the deal until it goes through and Resilient Financial sends out a press release."

"I see . . . Can you at least tell me what industry?"

"I can't tell you anything. The only thing I will tell you is that it is an industry that you need every day to live a healthy life."

Benjamin winces in pain and says, "That's enough information for me. It is about time for my medicine."

"Do you need me to get Linda?"

Benjamin nods as a look of pain spreads across his face. Kema hurries to the kitchen to get Linda. Linda returns to the master bedroom with an assortment of medication and a large glass of water. She props Benjamin's head up on two pillows before she gives him the medicine.

"I will leave now so that Daddy can get some rest," Kema says.

Benjamin's eyes are closed, signs of pain still on his face. Linda turns to Kema and says, "Thank you for stopping by. I know your father appreciates it."

EIGHTEEN

The weekend goes by quickly after her visit to Benjamin's house. After church on Sunday, Kema doesn't go to Janice's home for their usual Sunday dinner. Instead, she rushes back home to review the closing paperwork for the forward merger between Flemings International Foods and Unbelievable Foods. A forward merger is considered a simple transaction, because once Flemings International Foods acquires Unbelievable Foods, Unbelievable Foods will no longer be an independent entity. Although this merger is relatively straightforward, it is the first forward merger Kema has directed on her own, and the first one between such large corporations. Unbelievable Foods is a domestic, plant-based food company that sells the popular product Frikin Chicken. Flemings International Foods is the larger of the two companies and has the resources to market and distribute this product into international markets. It is a big deal, and she knows both her reputation and the reputation of her company is on the line. She wants to make sure that deal goes through smoothly, and that nothing goes wrong.

The merger closes in four days and any errors she notices in the paperwork on Sunday should be corrected by her staff no later than Tuesday. Thursday will be a busy day for Kema. The closing meeting is at nine in the morning. She told her mother that she would take her to her doctor's appointment that afternoon at three, and at seven Kema plans to take her team out to dinner to celebrate closing the deal. Just thinking about everything she has to do on Thursday makes her anxious yet excited because she is visualizing the final outcome: promotion to Managing Director.

Kema will be the first woman to be named Managing Director at Resilient Financial. She imagines herself speaking at events at the local high school and inspiring young women to pursue careers in the financial sector. She pictures herself making the 'Twenty Under Forty' features in national magazines and trade journals. Kema can even see Janice caring these publications to church with her to show her friends how much *her* daughter has achieved. Kema is modest by nature and would feel embarrassed by her mother flaunting her achievements, but she knows how much her mother has sacrificed for her and how much any victory she achieves is a victory for her mother, too. Although Janice occasionally annoys her, she knows that her mother made sacrifices to ensure that she was successful. A mother's pride about her child's accomplishments is undefeated.

Although Kema's alarm was set for 4:30 a.m., she wakes at 4:00 a.m. The day the merger will close has finally arrived. Kema leaps out of her bed, breezes through her morning workout, showers, and puts on her deal-closing outfit: a navy-blue Hugo Boss suit, white button-down shirt, and four-inch navy blue Prada pumps. Kema skips her morning cup of black tea and arrives to work at 6:30. She meets with her team for fifteen-minute review of the final details at 7:30 a.m. She can tell that her team is looking forward to closing the deal just as much as she is. They have been working at a fast pace for long hours over the past three months, and they are ready to see all their hard work pay off. When Kema returns to her desk, she quickly looks at her phone and notices a missed call and a voicemail from Linda. She plans to return Linda's call after the meeting because she thinks that Linda has only called to give her a status update on her father's condition. Moments later there is a knock at her door.

"Yes? Come in."

"Kema, I know you said you were not accepting personal calls until after two this afternoon, but a Mrs. Pérez says she needs to speak with you immediately." Kema briefly asks herself how Linda got her number, but by the tone of Marsha's voice, she can tell that something serious is going on and that she should accept the call.

"Transfer the call to my office, please" Kema says.

"Hello, this is Kema."

"Kema, you must come to Gorreta Hospital right away. Your father had another heart attack and is in critical condition."

"He has had multiple heart attacks before and has always pulled through. I am sure he will be fine. I will stop by the hospital this afternoon on my way home."

"I'm afraid if you don't come now that it might be too late."

Kema can tell by the shakiness in Linda's voice that this heart attack is different from his last heart attack. Kema says a five-second silent prayer and replies, "Ok, I'm on my way."

Kema runs out of her office to Marsha's desk.

"Marsha, can you contact our company helicopter pilot and tell him I need to get to Gorreta Hospital ASAP. Also, call Lauren McCullough and tell her that she will need to lead the meeting in my absence. I'll explain everything later. Right now, I just need to get on that helicopter!"

"I'll get right on it."

Kema thinks, *Of course Daddy would have a heart attack on one of the most important days in my life.* Kema does not know how understanding Mr. Flemings will be if she tells him she will not be present at the closing of this deal. Moreover, she has spent six months handling every detail of this deal to make the strongest possible case for her promotion from Director of Mergers and Acquisitions to Managing Director.

Kema closes her eyes and says, "Lord, I need you now!"

NINETEEN

Although the cabin of the helicopter is well airconditioned and cool, perspiration pours from Kema's underarms and forehead as she dials Mr. Flemings cell phone number. The phone rings twice before he answers.

"Hello?"

"Mr. Flemings, this is Kema Daniels. I wanted to let you know that I will not be able to attend the closing meeting today because my father is in critical condition in the hospital. As much as I want to be there to close the deal with you, I feel like I need to be with my father. Lauren McCullough, our Senior Merger and Acquisition Analyst, will preside over the closing meeting."

There is a five second pause before Mr. Flemings responds. "I'm very sorry to hear about your father. Thank you for letting me know. We will talk soon."

"I'm very sorry about this Mr. Flemings."

"Kema, please take care of yourself and your family."

"I will. Thank you."

Kema ends the call and looks out of the helicopter window searching for answers. Kema thinks, *God, I know you have a purpose and plan for everything in my life, but right now I feel confused.* She worries whether or not she has made the right decision to rush to the hospital knowing that she is missing a milestone meeting in her carefully planned career. As she gazes at the tops of buildings as they fly across the city, she contemplates how an innocent trip with a friend to Ladies' Night at a club has changed her life.

Before Kema can ponder any further, the helicopter lands on the rooftop of Gorreta Hospital. Kema disembarks quickly and takes the rooftop elevator down to the emergency room reception area. Once the elevator doors open, she sees Linda pacing back and forth, mascara running down her cheeks. Linda looks up mid pace to see Kema approaching.

Linda is too distraught for pleasantries and immediately starts telling Kema the sequence of events leading to Benjamin's current condition.

"Kema, he was fine when I left his room after giving him his medication. Five minutes later, I heard him screaming in pain. I ran to his room to see him clutching his chest. I called 911 . . . I'm really scared."

"You told me Daddy has survived three heart attacks. I'm sure he will make it through this one as well."

Linda looks down at the floor and shakes her head. "I . . . I should have stayed with him in the bedroom."

A doctor emerges from the critical care unit and approaches them.

"Mrs. Pérez can you please follow me? I need to speak to you in private."

Linda feels tightness in her throat and takes a few seconds before replying. "Dr. Richardson . . . can Kema join me? She is Benjamin's daughter."

"Yes, of course."

Linda and Kema follow Dr. Richardson into a small office directly across from the waiting room. When they enter, Kema notices a candy dish and a box of tissues on the table in the center of the room. There are two leather chairs on each side of the table.

"Please, have a seat," Dr. Richardson says with a stoic expression on his face.

Linda and Kema exchange glances before sitting in the chairs across from the doctor.

"I am sorry to be the bearer of bad news, but Mr. Daniels has died. We did all we could, but we just couldn't revive him. Mrs. Pérez, Kema, I'm very sorry for your loss."

Linda releases a guttural cry as if Dr. Richardson has punched her in the abdomen. Kema does her best to look stoically at Dr. Richardson, but she feels a solitary tear runs down her left cheek.

"I will give you two you some time to process this. Nurse Angela will come in fifteen minutes to take you to see Mr. Daniels."

Linda stops crying and begins rocking her upper body back and forth in the chair. "If I would have stayed in the bedroom a little longer, Ben would still be here."

Kema reaches for some tissues to hand to Linda. "This is not your fault. You did the best that you could."

Nurse Angela enters the room and tells Kema and Linda that they can each have time to see Benjamin. Kema hears her cell phone ringing in her purse and encourages Linda to go first. Nurse Angela escorts Linda out of the room. Kema looks at her phone and sees that Janice is calling her. In her haste to get to the hospital, Kema forgot to call her.

"Hello?"

"Kema, how did the meeting go? Are you coming to pick me up? I don't won't to be late for my doctor's appointment."

"No, Mama. I'm at Gorreta Hospital."

"Gorreta Hospital? Are you ok? What are you doing at a hospital?"

"Linda called me at work to tell me that Daddy was rushed to the hospital. Mama . . . the doctor just told us that Daddy died."

There is a long pause before Janice replies. "That man would go and die during the busiest time of your life. Did you at least attend the closing meeting?"

"No. I called Mr. Flemings and told him that I had a family emergency and that I would not be able to attend the meeting."

"You missed it? You may have ruined your chances of promotion by missing that meeting!"

"Mr. Flemings said he understood. Mama, I can't have this discussion right now."

"Fine. I will call the doctor's office and tell them I need to reschedule my appointment. Call me when you can talk."

Kema ends the call and puts her cell phone back in her purse. She thinks, *How could Mama be so insensitive?* Thirty minutes pass but it feels like an hour before Nurse Angela enters the room.

"Kema, you can see your father now."

Kema enters the room. Her father looks as if he is sleeping. No one prepares you for the day when you see your father lying on a bed he will never rise from again. Kema stops at the foot of the bed and begins talking to her father.

"Daddy, I thought we would have more time to get to know each other again. I thought I would invite you over to my place for dinner and that you would tease me about my cooking as you used to do with Mama. I thought you would eventually give me advice about how to find a good man. You were so passionate about your business, and I wanted to learn more about your future plans for Sweet Daddy's Fashions."

Tears start to flow from Kema's eyes. "I never got the chance to tell you that I never stopped loving you."

As she exits the room several minutes later, Kema sees Nurse Angela standing in the hall.

"Do you happen to know where Linda is?" Kema asks.

"Mrs. Pérez's sister came and took her home a few minutes ago. Mrs. Pérez wanted me to tell you to come to her home tomorrow morning at ten."

Kema nods her head in acknowledgement.

It is only three o'clock as Kema drives home from the hospital, but it feels as if she has put in a full day at work. Once home, she immediately kicks off her heels and drags herself up the stairs to her room. Kema uses her work phone and sends an email to her team to let them know that she will be out of the office for at least a week due to her father's death.

Kema has no appetite; she just wants to lie down. As soon as she reclines across her bed, she hears her cell phone ringing in her purse. She thinks, *Please don't let it be Mama. Of course—it's Mama.* Kema answers after the third ring.

"Hello?

"I rescheduled my doctor's appointment for next Tuesday. I guess I will have to ride the bus to it since you will likely be busy helping Ben's girlfriend with the funeral arrangements . . . Are you still at the hospital?"

"I'm at home now. Linda asked me to go over to her house tomorrow morning at ten."

"Why would you need to go to her house? Do you think that she wants to ask you to help pay for the burial? Do you think he had a will? If he did, I hope he left you something."

"Mama, I don't know why she wants me to come over. If you are so interested, you can come with me and find out for yourself."

"I don't want to step one foot in the house of that home-wrecker. But, you know that if you need my support, I'll come with you."

"Thank you, Mama. I will pick you up at 9:15."

TWENTY

Kema picks her mother up the following morning and they drive to Linda's house. Janice follows behind Kema as they approach the door. Kema rings the doorbell twice before Linda answers it. Linda looks at Kema with a weary smile and deep bags under her eyes. Linda can only see Kema when she says, "Hello, come on in."

Kema moves her body slightly and says, "Linda, I have brought my mother, Janice, with me."

Linda looks at Janice as if a dead enemy from her past has come back to life. Janice looks at her with a smirk before saying, "Hello".

Linda does not return her greeting. She simply opens the door wider. "Pardon me, please come in."

Kema and Janice follow Linda to the dining room and they all sit at the table. The table contains a massive document on legal size paper.

Linda looks across the table and addresses Kema. "After Benjamin had his second heart attack, he went to an estate lawyer and drafted a will. I wanted to discuss the will with you since I am the executioner of his estate. Then I'll let you read the document on your own."

Janice sucks her teeth in disgust before saying, "I had a feeling this meeting would be a set-up for some tomfoolery."

Kema looks at her mother with wide eyes, pleading for her to not cause trouble.

Linda ignores Janice's interruption and continues, "Benjamin gave me 50% of Sweet Daddy's Fashions and left the other 50% to you. I helped Benjamin establish Sweet Daddy's Fashions, but with him gone, I am not sure I want to run the business on my own. I think I'm ready to retire and spend more time with my family. I'd like to offer you the opportunity to buy my half of the business."

"Kema has a good career. What makes you think she wants any part of Sweet Daddy's Fashions?" Janice rudely inquires.

Linda sighs deeply before responding. "Benjamin wanted to leave a legacy for his family. He hoped and prayed that one day he would reunite with Kema and have something to give her."

"What else is he leaving you besides the business? You realize that we never divorced." Janice says spitefully.

"If you weren't so unforgiving towards Benjamin, he would have remained in your life. We were friends before we became lovers and life partners. I encouraged him to work it out with you after he lost his job and started drinking again. He told me that if he messed up one more time, you would kick him out of the house."

Janice is squinting her eyes at Linda as if she is a shooter who is focusing on a target. "You expect me to believe that you, an old stripper, told my husband to come back to me? You must think I was born last night. I saw the way you were teasing and flirting with him that night at the Player's Den. I *really* believe that you and him were just friends."

"You don't have to believe me, but I know that Benjamin made sure you were taken care of after he left you and Kema. Do you remember when you refused to accept his money when you were working at the diner?"

"Yeah, what's that got to do with anything?"

"Benjamin gave that money to your manager to give to you as a bi-weekly bonus."

Janice shakes her head in disbelief. "I worked hard for my bonuses at the diner! I treated my customers well."

"Benjamin knew you took pride in your job and didn't want any 'handouts.' This was the only way he knew to help support you and Kema."

Pools of water are in Janice's eyes and she looks as if she is trying to swallow a boulder. Kema goes into her purse to get some tissue and hands some to her mother. Janice takes the tissue, dabs her eyes, and turns silent.

Kema bursts into tears. "Mama, all this time I was thinking Daddy didn't care anything about us ... He wasn't there physically but he still cared ... He *still* cared!"

Linda feels as if she is going to cry again, but her eyes are all cried out. "Kema, let's meet at another time with the estate lawyer to discuss the details of the will. We need to work on an obituary for your father and discuss the funeral service. I don't know if you knew how much your father loved music. Before he died, he was working on a talent show for the community where the contestants could showcase their talents while wearing clothes from Sweet Daddy's Fashions. He was especially looking forward to highlighting the singer, Denise Lewis. Maybe we can see if she can sing at the service?"

Kema regains her composure and replies, "I think that would be a good idea. Do you have her number?"

"Yes, I'll text it to you."

Kema looks at Janice who is staring at an oil painting of a dancing couple on the wall. The man is wearing a fedora hat, white buttoned-down shirt, bowtie, and pants with suspenders. His right arm is wrapped around the waist of a woman wearing a gold camisole and black pencil skirt. The man's left arm is lifted in the air and his hand interlocked with the woman's hand. She wonders if her mother is reminiscing about her relationship with Benjamin's or feeling remorse that she never reconciled with him.

"Mama, I think we should leave and give Linda some space to grieve."

"Ok," Janice whispers as softly as if she were afraid to wake up an infant that had just fallen asleep.

Kema and Janice ride back to Janice's house in silence. Kema finally breaks the silence, "I understand seeing Linda brought back bad memories, but did you have to be so combative towards her?"

"I can't believe you are taking her side," Janice says as she turns her gaze from the car window to Kema. "You do realize that she is the reason why your father left us."

"I'm not taking a side. It seems to me that I don't even know the whole story. You never told me that he came to the diner after you saw him at the Player's Den."

"You were too young to understand what goes on between a husband and a wife. I would have ––"

"I asked you about my father many times when I was an *adult*, but––"

"Kema, that man and his girlfriend were dead to me a long time ago. I buried them so I could focus on raising you. His funeral will just be a formality to me."

"Are you being serious right now? Didn't you teach me the importance of forgiveness?"

"I thought I had forgiven him, but seeing Linda again made me remember the night I saw them together at the Player's Den. *She* got to have the relationship that I was supposed to have with your father."

"Holding on to this bitterness is only going to make you feel worse."

"I know this, Kema. I had forgiven him in my mind, but my heart still hurts."

Kema drops her Mama off at her house and promises to call her later in the day to check in. Before Kema drives away, she looks at her cell phone and sees a text from Linda.

Hi Kema. Denise Lewis number is 773-801-2957

TWENTY-ONE

Kema decides to call Denise Lewis as soon as she gets home. The phone rings four times before the call is answered by a woman with a voice that sounds like her vocal cords had been scratched by ten cats.

"Hello?"

"Hello, is this Denise?"

"This is she . . ."

"My name is Kema Daniels. I'm Benjamin Daniels' daughter. Linda Pérez gave me your number."

"Ok . . ."

"I don't know how best to say this, but my father passed away yesterday."

"What? Is this a prank call? How do I know you are who you say you are and are telling the truth? Sweet Daddy, I mean Mr. Ben, never said he had a daughter . . ."

Kema takes a breath before responding. "I hadn't seen my father in almost twenty-five years before we reunited a few weeks ago. But that isn't why I am calling. I'm calling to ask if you would be able to sing at his funeral. I was told that he really enjoyed listening to you sing."

"Mr. Ben heard me sing at Amateur Night at the Player's Den two months ago. He came up to me and told me that I had a soulful voice and that he would like me to perform in a talent show he was planning. He said he wanted the talent show to happen every year to showcase Chicago-area talent. He really cared about the community and wanted to help us shine like stars. I guess the talent show isn't going to happen now. I'm really sorry to hear he has passed away. I would be honored to sing at the funeral, even if I have to call in sick at work to do so."

"Thank you, Denise. I will call you as soon as I have more details about the location and time of the service."

No one has called Kema to tell her what happened at the closing meeting. She assumes her team is giving her time and space to deal with her personal issues without burdening her with work. As busy as she is with family matters, Kema hasn't forgotten about the deal—and how much is at stake for her in it. She wants an update on the meeting so she dials Lauren McCullough, her Senior Merger and Acquisition Analyst, to find out how it went.

"Hello, this is Lauren."

"Hello, Lauren it's Kema. How are you?"

"I'm doing well. I didn't think I would hear from you so soon. My sincere condolences. Let me know if there is anything I can do."

"Thank you for that, Lauren. But the reason I'm calling is to get your thoughts on how the closing meeting went."

"We outlined our plan to merge the finances of Flemings International Foods and Unbelievable Foods. We emphasized that we were there to support both organizations during every phase of the process. Mr. Flemings seemed pleased with the presentation and the overall plan. He said that he would provide feedback to our CEO that will highlight your dedication and professionalism throughout the deal."

"Thank you for stepping in for me, Lauren. I am happy to hear that everything went smoothly."

"Please let me know if there is anything, I can do for you while you are out of the office."

"Thank you, again."

Kema is happy that her team was successful without her there, though she can't help feeling slightly resentful that Lauren served as the team lead for one of the most important meetings in *her* career. Maybe she should call Mr. Flemings to get his feedback directly. Surely, he would not mind hearing from her. She finds his number and calls him.

"Edward Flemings speaking."

"Hello, Mr. Flemings, this is Kema Daniels."

"Hello, Kema. How are you? Marsha told me that your father died. My deepest condolences to you and your family."

"Thank you, Mr. Flemings. I'm doing ok. The purpose of my call is to find out if you had any questions or feedback for me now that deal has closed."

"I do have one question for you. Why are you worried about the deal and not spending this time with your loved ones? You prepared your team well, and they successfully addressed all of our concerns during the meeting. You are a dynamic leader, Ms. Daniels, and I look forward to speaking with the CEO of your firm to highly recommend you for promotion."

"That is very kind of you. Thank you."

"Ms. Daniels, can I ask one more question?"

"Of course, Mr. Flemings."

"Did you get to spend some time with your father before he died?"

Kema gulps before responding. "Not as much as I would have liked. After my dinner with him and his girlfriend, I only saw him when he returned home from the hospital after his heart attack. But, even though the visit was short, I was able to see that he still had a sense of humor and learn how much passion he had for his business."

"Do you know who will take over the business?"

"His will directs that half of the business be given to me and the other half to his girlfriend."

"Are you considering honoring his will?"

"I am not sure. I don't want to commit to anything that might jeopardize my career."

"That is very reasonable, Ms. Daniels. In spite of his shortcomings as a father, it sounds like your father led a full life. Now it is up to you to figure out what kind of life you want to lead."

"Thank you, Mr. Flemings. I will keep that in mind."

"Love, life, and laughter to you Ms. Daniels."

"Same to you, Mr. Flemings."

TWENTY-TWO

The next morning, Kema sleeps in until she hears her cell phone ringing. It's Linda calling to ask if she can come over to her house at one o'clock to meet with her and the estate lawyer. Kema agrees. Linda then asks her if she plans on bringing Janice. Kema assures her that Janice will stay at home this time. Linda breathes an audible sigh of relief.

Kema notices a gunmetal grey colored BMW 750i parked in front of Linda's house. Kema thinks the car must belong to the estate lawyer. She wonders how much money her father had if he could pay for an expensive lawyer's services. Kema parks across the street and walks toward the door. Linda must have been looking out the window because Linda opens the door for Kema before she reaches the house. Linda looks more rested than she did the previous day. She is wearing makeup and a burgundy blouse with black slacks. Linda guides Kema to the dining room table where the estate lawyer is sitting.

"Kema, this is Victor Pennington, Benjamin's estate lawyer."

"Hello, Kema. It is a pleasure to meet you."

Kema takes a while to respond. She is captivated by Victor. He is six-feet three-inches tall with a slim, muscular build that his tailored gray suit complements well. His hair is cut close to his scalp, he has a chestnut colored complexion, and sports a goatee which complements his perfectly white teeth. Kema scans for a wedding band on his left hand and does not see one.

She thinks, *Not having a wedding band doesn't mean anything; he could be in a relationship or even engaged.*

"Nice to meet you, Mr. Pennington."

"You can call me Victor. Mr. Pennington is my father."

"I'll keep that in mind." Kema can't help but grin at Victor's attempt at humor.

"Now that we have been introduced, here is your copy of the will. I'll give you a chance to review it and then I'll answer any questions that you have."

Kema notices that the will has a table of contents. She flips to the "Due Diligence" section of the will and notes that in the event of Linda's untimely death, Mr. Pennington would become the executor. Kema thinks, *Daddy trusts this man so much that he would allow him to execute his will?*

"Mr. . . . I mean...Victor. How long have you known my father?"

"I have known him for six years, I met him at a networking event in the Loop. I complemented him on his suit, and the next thing I knew, he was telling me all about Sweet Daddy's Fashions. Since then, I have purchased plenty of suits and casual outfits from his store. I told him that when he was ready to create his will, he should come to me. I was pleasantly surprised when he finally took me up on my offer. He said it was the least that he could do considering how much money I had spent at Sweet Daddy's Fashions."

"It sounds like you had a great relationship with my father."

"I like to think we did, though I didn't know that he had a daughter—you—until I started assisting him with his will. He made it clear to me that, though he hadn't been present in your life, he would leave a legacy for you. Now, I can see for myself why that was so important to him."

Kema smiles and can feel her face getting warm and her body temperature rising as if someone has turned on the heat. She quickly looks back at the will to try to regain composure.

Kema then turns to the "Personal Property and Assets" section. Linda was correct when she told her that she would receive 50% of Sweet Daddy's Fashions. Kema looks further down the page and notices that her mother's name is also in the will.

> To my estranged wife, Janice Lorraine Daniels, I leave the sum of $25,000 (twenty-five thousand dollars).

"My mother is named is in the will." Kema says in disbelief.

"That is correct. Can you provide me with her address so I can mail a copy of the will to her as well as instructions on how to collect the funds?"

"Mama is not going to believe this."

Kema finishes reading the will and then gives Victor her mother's address.

"Thank you, Kema. I will see you at the funeral service. If you have any questions for me, you can contact me here." Victor says as he hands her his business card.

"Thank you, Victor." Kema replies.

Victor shakes her hand before Linda escorts him to the door. He turns back and waves at Kema. Kema thinks, *Busted . . . How did he know that I was watching him leave?*

Linda returns to the dining room and she and Kema go over the details of the funeral service. Kema tells Linda that she spoke with Denise Lewis who has agreed to sing at the funeral service. Linda pulls out a photo album of special moments at Sweet Daddy's Fashions from which she and Kema select a few pictures for the program.

"This is a picture of your father at the grand opening of Sweet Daddy's Fashions," says Linda.

"You can see the ambition and pride in his eyes," replies Kema.

Kema looks through the other pictures in the album and finds a picture of him with Darron, both of them wearing black business suits as they stand in front of the store counter. "I think this would be a nice photo to include in the program."

"I agree. Darron adored Benjamin. When I called to tell him that Benjamin had died, he asked if he could speak during the service." Linda pauses before she speaks again. "I only have pictures of Benjamin from our life together. Do you think your mother saved any pictures of him?"

"I don't know, but I will ask her."

"We have only two days to finalize the program. Since Benjamin served in the Army, I arranged for him to be buried at Lincoln Cemetery."

"I'll stop by Mama's house today and let you know."

When Kema leaves Linda's house, she calls her mother to tell her that she will stop by her house. She thinks, *Mama is going to faint when she finds out that Daddy included her in his will. I wish I could record her reaction.*

Kema tells her mother about the money designated for her in the will.

"He left me how much?" Janice asks in astonishment.

"$25,000." Kema replies.

"Are you sure that you read it right? Janice asks again. You know that you have been putting off going to the eye doctor."

"I'm certain. Victor, I mean the estate lawyer, is the one who told me that you are included in the will. I gave him your address so he can send you a copy of the will and instructions on how to obtain the money."

Janice shakes her head in disbelief and says, "I need to see this with my own eyes."

"Mama, do you have any old pictures of Daddy? We want to use some old photos of him in the funeral program."

"I haven't looked at pictures of your father in over thirty years. I threw away his clothes a long time ago but, I think I still have some pictures under the bed."

Janice and Kema go to the bedroom. Janice pulls out an old black shoe box with the top worn away. Inside the box is a photo album with pictures of Benjamin going all the way back to his childhood. The first picture in the album is of him in elementary school.

Janice shakes her head and laughs. "He had that same smile the day I met him at the diner. He didn't talk much about his childhood when he was with me, but I bet he was a charmer back then, too."

The next picture in the album is of him in his Army uniform standing at attention. "This will be a great picture to include in the program," Kema says.

As they flip through the album, they stop on a picture of Kema and Benjamin holding hands. Kema looks to be around six years old and she is looking up at Benjamin with a smile. "I took this picture after you and your father came home from one of your many trips to the corner store," says Janice.

"I think I remember this. I really want to include this picture in the program." Kema says as she turns her gaze from the picture and looks at her mother. "Mama, about the other day at Linda's house . . . I think you owe her an apology."

"I have been thinking about that day. I prayed about it and I know that I need to apologize. But first, I want to apologize to you for not telling you the truth about your father. I should not have let my issues and my feeling of abandonment affect your relationship with him. When you told me that you wanted to reunite and get to know him, I was scared. I was afraid that he would say something about me that would turn you against me. I couldn't take not having you in my life."

Kema has tears in her eyes. "Mama, you worked so hard to provide for us. You are the biggest part of my support system. I would never turn against you."

Kema and Janice embrace and begin weeping tears that have been bottled up for years. The tears seem to wash away the suppressed hurt and resentment they shared between them. Kema wipes her eyes with the back of her hand and looks at her mother. They smile at each other and know everything will be alright.

TWENTY-THREE

The morning before Benjamin's funeral, Kema is feeling anxious because she is uncertain if her mother will give a sincere apology to Linda after the funeral service. Kema knows if she calls and asks Janice about it again it will only irritate her. One thing that Kema has learned over the years is that there is a direct relationship between irritation and anxiety: once Janice is irritated, Kema's anxiety increases. Kema is also anxious about work. Mr. Flemings assured her that he would provide positive feedback to management about his experience with Kema and her team, but she has no way of knowing how this feedback will influence whether or not upper management decides to promote her.

Before she can dive into the hypotheticals of what might happen, her company phone rings. Kema doesn't recognize the number, but she answers the phone anyway.

"Hello, this is Kema Daniels."

"Ms. Daniels, this is Trevor Reynolds. How are you this morning?"

Kema's eyes widen to the size of golf balls and her mouth hangs open. *Trevor Reynolds, the CEO of Resilient Financial has called her.*

"Hello, Ms. Daniels, are you there?"

"Yes, I'm sorry. I'm here Mr. Reynolds. How can I be of service?"

"Ms. Daniels, first I want to say that I'm sorry for your loss."

"Thank you, Mr. Reynolds."

"The other day I had the opportunity to speak with Mr. Flemings regarding his experience with you and your team. He said that you exhibited excellent leadership throughout the process, and he hopes to be able to work with you again in the future. Unfortunately, I had to tell him that he would not be able to work with you again."

Kema's felt as if she had just been kicked in the gut. Is Mr. Reynolds calling to tell her that she is being fired? She tells herself to breath and respond professionally.

"Mr. Reynolds, may I ask why I will not be working with Mr. Flemings again?"

"Ms. Daniels, you have been an asset to our organization for over ten years. I think it would be unfair to you—or to the firm—if we kept you as Director of Mergers and Acquisitions. That is why I'm offering you the position of Managing Director of Mergers and Acquisitions. I know this is a difficult time for you right now, and you may not feel in the best position to make such an important decision. That is why I think you should take some time to consider my offer. You can give me your decision next week."

Kema thinks she will burst with all the emotion pent up inside of her. She takes a few deep breaths to steady herself before she speaks. "Thank you so much, Mr. Reynolds. I'm honored that you and the board are considering me for this position. I have a lot going on with my family at the moment, but I promise that I will get back to you shortly."

"It was my pleasure to deliver this news. Enjoy the rest of your morning."

Kema double-checks that she has ended the call and then she runs through her condo in excitement. As Managing Director of Mergers and Acquisitions she would be responsible for bringing in new clients for Resilient Financial and developing the corporate vision for the Mergers and Acquisitions department. It is everything she has been working so hard to achieve for as long as she can remember; her career dream has finally come true. Should she call her mother and let her know or should she call her best friend Sharon first? Her mother will give her anxiety and asks a bunch of follow up questions she has no interest in answering, whereas Sharon will be nothing but excited for her. She decides to call Sharon first.

"Hello?"

"Girl, you will not believe who just called me?"

"Who called? I hope it isn't more bad news. You don't need it right now, Kema."

"Mr. Reynolds, the CEO of Resilient Financial called and offered me the position of Managing Director of Mergers and Acquisition!"

"Oh, my goodness. That is great news. Congratulations, Kema! You have been working so hard for this promotion."

"Thank you. I have until next week to officially accept the position."

"What did Mama Janice say when you told her?"

"You're the first person I've told. I'm gonna call her next."

"What? I feel honored to be the first. Don't forget about your girl when you appear for interviews with Oprah and are in the issues of *Fast Company* for being the first female CEO of Resilient Financial."

Kema laughs. She can always count on Sharon to lighten her mood. "I won't forget about you. I will need you to maintain my professional appearance for all those photoshoots I'll be having."

"I'll hold you to it. Don't go changing your number on me."

"I won't. I need to tell *you* not to change your number. You already have two salons in Chicago and are working on a third."

"No matter how many salons I have, I will always make time for my best friend."

"Thank you, Sharon. I should probably call Mama now. I'll see you tomorrow at the funeral."

After she ends her call with Sharon, Kema calls her mother to tell her the good news.

"Good morning, Mama. How are you?"

"I'm doing ok this morning. How are you, baby?"

"I got some good news this morning. The CEO of Resilient Financial called and offered me the Managing Director of Mergers and Acquisition position!"

"Congratulations! I'm so proud of you, baby. I told you that all of your hard work would pay off. Did you accept the position?"

"No. He told me that due to my family situation, he wanted me to take a week before letting them know."

"Kema, what are you waiting on? You have worked ten long years to get to this level. I would have told him yes immediately . . . Wait . . . Are you thinking about rejecting this offer?"

Kema rolls her eyes and takes a deep breath before replying. "This has been an emotional couple of weeks for me, and I just need some time to clear my mind to make the right decision."

"Ok . . . I just hope you are not stalling because you are thinking about your 50% ownership of your father's little clothing store."

Kema decides to change the subject. "Mama, I would like to be at Linda's tomorrow morning by nine, so I will pick you up at 8:30. Will you be ready? The funeral procession will leave Linda's at 9:30. We will ride in the limousine with Linda, her sister, Camila, and Linda's niece, Jasmine."

"Ok, I'll be ready."

TWENTY-FOUR

When Kema and Janice arrive at Linda's house at around 9:15 the next morning they see seven police officers on motorcycles, two limousines, and three cars in front of the house. The police officers greet Kema and Janice as they walk up to the door. Camila opens the door for them.

"Hello. Please come in, we have been waiting for you. We thought you would be here earlier to eat breakfast with the family." Camila says with more than a hint of annoyance.

"I'm so sorry, Camila, I didn't know that you all planned to have breakfast or I would have come earlier." Kema then quickly introduces her mother to Camila. "Mama, this is Camila, Linda's sister."

"Nice to meet you," Janice says, attempting to sound sincere.

"Likewise," Camila replies, giving Janice a look that lets her know that she has heard plenty of disparaging gossip about her. "I think you may only have time for a little coffee before we have to get in the limousine."

"I'm more of a tea drinker. Mama, would you like some coffee?" Kema asks.

Janice's first inclination is to refuse anything this woman offers her, but then she remembers that she is supposed to be on her best behavior. She puts on her best pleasant smile before replying, "Yes, I would love a cup of coffee with cream, but no sugar, please, if it will not be too much trouble."

Camila returns Janice's smile with a half-hearted smile before going into the kitchen. Janice and Kema are in the living room and the smell of freshly brewed coffee mixed in with ham teased both of their nostrils. They hear Linda's family members speaking Spanish in the kitchen and they sound as if they are enjoying themselves.

A few moments pass before she reemerges from the kitchen with a Styrofoam cup with a lid. Linda is following closely behind her.

Camila hands Janice the coffee. Janice thanks Camila.

"Hello, ladies." Linda says to Kema and Janice, "We have five minutes before we need to get in the limousine to go to the funeral home. If you need to go to the bathroom, you should go now. The guest bathroom is the first door on the left."

Kema excuses herself to use the bathroom and leaves Janice in the living room with Linda and Camila.

"This coffee is good. What's the name of the brand?" Janice asks to break the silence.

"It's called El Coqui." Linda replies, "It is a Puerto Rican brand."

"El Co..what?" Janice replies.

"El Co-key" Linda repeats the words awkwardly. "Ok, thanks. Where can I buy it?"

"It's available in every supermarket in Puerto Rico, but I get it online. I have an order coming in soon so I can give you what I have left in the kitchen."

Janice is taken aback by Linda's generosity and now is feeling extremely guilty for her past behavior towards her. "Thank you . . . Linda . . . This is hard for me, but I want to apologize for being rude to you in your own home the other day. I realize that you and Benjamin shared a special bond. My time with him was only for a season. I was jealous because you were able to see him become the man that I always knew he could be."

Linda walks closer to Janice and embraces her. Kema returns to the living room just in time to see Linda and Janice hugging. The sight of these women who were once enemies now comforting each other brings her to tears.

TWENTY-FIVE

Linda, Kema, Janice, and Camila get in the first limousine. Jasmine, and two aunts and two uncles are riding in the second limousine. Linda's other nieces and nephews ride in the other three cars. The police officers lead the caravan of cars to the funeral home, stopping all other traffic on their way. As the caravan turns the corner onto the street where the funeral home is located, Kema looks out the window and sees cars parked on both sides of the street and at least fifty people walking towards the funeral home. It appears the entire community has come out to attend the funeral. Linda is curious as to what is holding Kema's attention and looks out the window as well. A faint smile appears on her weary face as she sees for the first time how many people have come to honor pay their respects.

The limousine drivers park in the circular driveway and open the doors for the family members to exit. The funeral director greets the family in the lobby and gives the final instructions on how the funeral procession will go. The family walks in pairs: Kema and Linda at the head of the line, Janice and Camila right behind them. A piano player is playing the song "Blessed Assurance." Kema notices Victor Pennington standing on the left side of the chapel which has been designated for close friends of the family. He nods at her and smiles. His small gesture comforts Kema. Kema quickly scans the funeral chapel for Sharon. She doesn't see her, but assumes she will see her at the cemetery.

The family is seated in the front of the chapel facing Benjamin's bronze casket, which is surrounded by an assortment of beautiful and fragrant flowers. Denise Lewis, Benjamin's favorite local singer, approaches the casket to sing a song to pay her respect.

Before Denise sings her song, she addresses the attendees. "I am going to miss Mr. Daniels. I met him right after I sang a song at the Player's Den. I was feeling bad that night because I thought it would be my last time singing in front of an audience. I was working long hours at my job and worried I would not be able to find the time to sing. Benjamin told me that he loved my singing and that I should keep going no matter. He told me it would be tough and take a lot of sacrifice, but that I had a talent that I could not give up on. I believe God sent him into my life at the perfect time to give me hope and encourage me. I hope this song I'm about to sing encourages all of you as well."

Denise's alto voice fills the chapel and moves everyone to tears when she sings:

"God is, the joy and the strength of my life . . . He removes all pain, misery and strife, He promises to keep you, never to leave you, He'll never ever come short of his word . . ."

After Denise's song, Darron walks to the front of the chapel to share how Benjamin impacted his life.

"Instead of judging me for hanging out with my friends on the corner, Mr. Daniels offered me a job. Most adults would have called the police if they saw us hanging around the way we did. Not Mr. Daniels. He was a problem solver and was always coming up with ways in which he could help the people in our community. He had so many ideas for how to make our community a better place. I hope that as I work on my business degree, I can also work to implement his ideas and improve our community. What we build from the foundation he laid for us will be his true legacy."

The intensity of the moment is too much for Linda to bear and the grief hits her hard. Her emotions are finally catching up with her. She begins sobbing and Kema hands her tissue while Camila holds tightly to her left hand.

Janice keeps her head lowered throughout the service until Alderman Peter Simpson comes to the front of the chapel. She turns to Kema and whispers, "How did your father know Alderman Simpson? That man never met a stranger."

"For those of you who do not know me, I'm Alderman Peter Simpson of Ward 11. I met Benjamin five years ago after a city council meeting when he asked me what the council planned to do about the increase in youth crime. I told him that we were working on a solution that we would share with the public soon. Benjamin was not satisfied with my answer and offered me his own proposal on combating youth crime. He proposed a partnership between the City of Chicago and all the businesses located in the ward that would provide jobs and job training for the young people of the community. I told him that this proposal sounded good but was unrealistic. He countered my resistance by saying that he would start small by implementing a one-year pilot program with the businesses on Roosevelt Road. Benjamin shared the results of the pilot program to the council two weeks ago and the council voted this week to expand the program to all of Ward 11."

Everyone in the chapel erupts in applause.

Alderman Simpson continues, "Last but not least, after hearing of Benjamin's untimely passing, the council held an emergency session to vote for changing the name of the block of Roosevelt Road on which Sweet Daddy's Fashions is located to Benjamin Daniel's Way."

The funeral home erupts in applause again. Kema and Janice embrace and then turn to embrace Linda.

When the funeral service ends, everyone returns to their vehicles to be led by the seven police officers on motorcycles to the Lincoln Cemetery. Exiting the limousine at the cemetery, Kema sees Sharon. They embrace and walk together towards the committal service shelter for the bestowing of military funeral honors and the internment of the coffin. Once the family and friends are seated, one uniformed serviceperson plays *Taps* on a bugle while the two other uniformed servicepersons stand at attention. When the song ends, the two uniformed servicepersons fold the flag. One uniformed service person hands Kema the flag and says, "On behalf of the President of the United States, the United States Army, and a grateful Nation, please accept this flag as a symbol of our appreciation for your loved one's honorable and faithful service."

Kema's head is bowed as she accepts the flag. Sharon is sitting beside her and gently squeezes her shoulder. They are both crying.

As Sharon walks with Kema back to the limousine, she tells Kema that she has to take care of business at one of her salons and will not be able to attend the repast. Kema appreciates that Sharon was able to be with her, even if only for a short time.

Now that the funeral ceremonies have ended, Benjamin's family and friends drive to an event center for the repast. The food—which consists of fried chicken, macaroni and cheese, turnip greens, arroz con pollo, plantains, pound cake, and flan to represent both African-American and Puerto-Rican culture—is served buffet style. Some of the friends who had arrived earlier are sitting at the tables excitedly discussing the block name being changed to honor Benjamin.

The first person Kema sees as she walks through the door is Victor. He is smiling at her and makes a hand motion that signals he wants her to sit with him. Kema waves back at him and Janice looks at both Kema and Victor suspiciously. Janice follows Kema to his table to investigate. Victor stands up when they get to the table and pulls out two chairs for them to sit in.

"Hello, Victor, it is nice to see you again. Mama, this is Victor Pennington, the estate lawyer I was telling you about."

Victor extends his hand to Janice. "It is very nice to meet you, Mrs. Daniels."

"It is nice to meet you Mr. Pennington," Janice says as she shakes his hand. "I hear that you convinced Benjamin to leave me some money in his will," Janice adds sarcastically.

Victor is not phased. "I put him in a choke hold and told him that he had to leave something to you for all the pain and suffering he caused."

Janice laughs. "Mr. Pennington, I don't believe you at all. Benjamin would not have given you a chance to put him in a choke hold. He was stubborn and moved too quickly."

"Benjamin was a mover and a shaker and a proud man. He wanted to make sure his family was taken care of financially." Victor takes out a business card and hands it to Janice. "If you have any questions, please contact me."

Janice takes the card and studies it before she places it in her purse. Victor rises from his seat and says, "I'm going up to the buffet. Would you ladies like me to bring you anything?"

"Thank you for the offer, Victor." Kema replies, "We will join the buffet line soon."

When Janice thinks Victor is far enough away from the table not to hear their conversation, she exclaims, "He sure was excited to see you . . . and you seemed excited to see him. I thought you told me you just met him at Linda's house."

"Yes, Mama. This is only my second time seeing him."

"Watch him and tread lightly. He is smooth and confident like your Daddy."

"What's wrong with him being smooth and confident?"

"Nothing, if you don't mind sharing him with other women."

"He could just be friendly and outgoing. Besides, what makes you think that he is interested in me? He could have a girlfriend or could even be married."

"I have studied people long enough in the diner to know when a man is interested. Just remember what I told you, Kema."

After the repast, Kema and Janice return to Linda's house to take some of the flowers and the El Coqui coffee for Janice. It is eight o'clock at night when Kema arrives back at her condo and she is exhausted. She kicks off her shoes at the door and does not bother to take them upstairs with her. She places the lilies she took from Linda's house on her windowsill. Kema's mind is reeling as she ponders the day's events while she lies in bed. She realizes that her father has left a legacy. The number of people who came to the funeral to pay their respect was overwhelming. Her Daddy had made such a significant impact on the entire community that the city council voted to name a block after him. Kema remembers Linda's offer to sell Kema her share of the business. Kema asks herself, *What do I know about running a clothing store? I should just stick to my career plan. Darron is will be more than able to buy Linda's portion in a few years.*

After tossing and turning for what feels like hours, Kema manages to fall asleep only to be awakened suddenly by her cell phone ringing.

"Hello?"

"Kema, this is Linda. Are you sleeping?"

"Yes, I was sleeping. Is everything alright?"

"The alarm company just called me and told me that the store alarm was set off and they think there might have been a break in. They have dispatched the police to check it out. Can you meet me there?"

"Of course. I'll be there in about twenty minutes."

Kema ends the call and thinks to herself, *The thugs didn't even have enough respect to wait until the day after Daddy's funeral to break into the store. Daddy, I know you meant well by leaving me half of your store, but I didn't sign up for this.*

TWENTY-SIX

Kema parks across the street from the store. She exits her car and sees a crowd of over a hundred people and four policemen outside the store. Kema can't detect any obvious signs that a burglary has occurred. As she approaches the store window, she sees that people have placed flowers and colorful ties outside the store window and door. A few people in the crowd are shaking their heads in disgust and she overhears a man who looks to be in his late fifties telling another man who looks to be around the same age that the neighborhood will go downhill now that Sweet Daddy has died.

As she passes the two men, she tells them, "Don't worry, we will not let what happened tonight ruin all the progress that my father made in this neighborhood."

One of the men asks her, "Are you running for Alderman or something?"

"No, I'm Sweet Daddy's daughter," replies Kema as she walks on without breaking her stride.

"Sweet Daddy's daughter?" The men ask in unison.

When Kema gets to the door, she sees Linda, who greets her with a weary smile.

"Kema, I'm sorry to get you out of bed for this. Some people who weren't able to make it to the funeral this afternoon decided to hold their own memorial service for your father here at his store. The police think the alarm was triggered because so many people were so close to the front door and the window."

Kema is relieved that the store has not been burglarized and is overwhelmed once again by the community's reverence and appreciation for her father.

Darron sees her and Linda in the crowd and walks over to them. "Hi, Ms. Kema. I'm sorry I didn't get a chance to speak to you after the funeral today."

"That's alright . . ." Kema pauses, "Did you know there was going to be a gathering tonight?"

"Yeah . . . I mean yes . . . A lot of people had to work this afternoon and couldn't make it to the funeral. I sent a message through the store's Instagram account letting our followers know that we would gather at the store at nine to pay tribute to your father. Not that many people liked the post, so I didn't think that many people would show up."

Kema shakes her head slowly. "I wish you would have told me or Ms. Linda about this. We could have helped you plan this event for another day."

Before Darron can respond, a news reporter and a cameraman from ABC7 run towards them. The news reporter has a microphone in her hand and places it in Darron's face.

The reporter asks, "Are you responsible for the crowd that has gathered here tonight in memory of Mr. Benjamin Daniels?"

Darron looks at Kema and Linda before responding. Both give him confirmation by nodding at him. "Yes, I am. It was important to me that the community acknowledge Mr. Daniels for the role model he has been, not just to me, but to so many others. Even so, I'm surprised by how many people have come out."

"I looked at older posts on the store's Instagram account and saw that Mr. Daniels was planning on hosting a fashion and talent show in two weeks. Now that Mr. Daniels is no longer with us, will there still be a show?"

"Yes, the fashion and talent show will take place as scheduled." Kema replies without hesitation.

"Well, you heard it here first. This is Megan Williams reporting from Sweet Daddy's Fashions."

Megan asks for Kema and Darron's full name to place in the chyron for the news story. She tells them to watch the eleven o'clock news to see the story.

Kema and Linda look at Darron who is grinning from ear to ear as if Megan just told him that he won the lottery.

"We made the news! Darron exclaims. We may even go viral once I place the news clip on our Instagram page."

"I think I have had enough excitement for the day." Linda says. "Darron, can you be responsible for cleaning up after the memorial? We will keep the store closed for the weekend, but we will reopen on Monday. Be sure to post the change in hours on the door and on all our social media accounts."

"Yes, Ma'am," Darron replies.

TWENTY-SEVEN

Saturday and Sunday race by in a blur, and before she knows it, Kema finds herself driving to work on Monday morning. Today is the day that she will formally accept the position of Managing Director of Mergers and Acquisitions. Her meeting with Trevor Reynolds is scheduled for 9:00 a.m., and Kema is relieved that the meeting is early in the day to allow her to focus on her other tasks at work. She knows if it was at the end of the day, she would have trouble thinking about anything other than the meeting.

Kema passes Marsha's desk on the way to her office. "Welcome back, Kema!" Marsha greets her cheerfully.

"Thank you, Marsha. I'm happy to be back at work. I hope you haven't been too overwhelmed in my absence."

"It's been fine. Everyone here has been very patient and understanding in your absence. The only update I have for you is that your meeting with Mr. Reynolds has been pushed back to 9:30 a.m. and will now be in the main conference room with the Board of Directors"

"Thank you, Marsha."

Kema decides to use the extra time in her office to check her email and drink a cup of mint tea. The extra time is good because it allows her to compose herself before the meeting.

Kema arrives in the conference room ten minutes before the meeting is set to begin to find that two of the five members of the Board of Directors are already in the room. Kema shakes their hands and takes the first seat on the right side of the table. Moments later, Mr. Reynolds and the remaining members arrive.

"Ms. Daniels, thank you for meeting with us this morning. I know this is your first day back at work after the death of your father, and we wanted to once again offer you our deepest condolences."

"Thank you for your kind words and understanding during this difficult time. I feel lucky to work with such empathetic colleagues."

"We are grateful to have you working with us hope that you will be playing even more of a role at the company in the years to come by accepting the position of Managing Director of Mergers and Acquisitions."

"I am honored to be considered for this position. I have had some time to think about the offer over the last week, and with humility and gratefulness that I accept the promotion to Managing Director of Mergers and Acquisitions."

"We are pleased that you are accepting this promotion. We have scheduled a working lunch today from noon until two to go over your new duties and responsibilities. You can retain your current executive assistant, or you have the option to select a virtual executive assistant who is familiar with your new role. This new position requires a significant amount of travel since you will be the face of your department and on the Resilient Financial leadership team."

"I look forward to working through all the details over lunch."

"Great! We will travel to the restaurant in corporate cars. Please meet us in the lobby at 11:30."

"I will see you there. Thank you again for this incredible opportunity."

TWENTY-EIGHT

A father will hold his daughter's hand for a time but will hold her heart for eternity.

Over her lunch with Board of Directors, Kema not only learns more about the new role she will be assuming at the firm, but also that Lauren McCullough will be promoted to Kema's previous position after successfully leading the final meeting between Flemings International Food and Unbelievable Foods. Lauren will move into Kema's office while Kema will move into an office on the top floor that overlooks Lake Michigan. Kema's learns that her new role will involve significantly less hands-on project management and many meetings with private equity and venture capital firms. It will be her responsibility to persuade them to allow Resilient Financial to manage their investment portfolios and handle their mergers and acquisitions.

She learns as well that Resilient Financial is expanding into the technology, energy, and healthcare sectors and will need the Directors of Mergers & Acquisitions to manage these new interests. Kema will meet frequently with the Directors of Mergers & Acquisitions to strategize how to bring more business to Resilient Financial.

When Kema returns from lunch, she tells her executive assistant Marsha about the details of her new position. Kema explains to Marsha that due to the frequent traveling involved with her new position, it ordinarily requires a virtual assistant but offers her the opportunity to continue working with her.

To Kema's surprise, Marsha decides to remain in her current role, meaning she will become Lauren McCullough's executive assistant. Marsha explains to Kema that she is comfortable with her current duties and responsibilities. She would have to learn new software if she were to move upstairs with Kema, and she is not sure she is willing to take on such a difficult task.

Although Kema is disappointed that Marsha will no longer be her assistant, Kema is excited for the opportunities that lie ahead of her. She has reached her career goal of becoming a Managing Director and anticipates her mother's joy when she tells her that she has formally accepted the position. She plans to call her after she leaves work for the day. Kema promised herself that she would not get distracted at work. The past few weeks have provided enough distraction.

While Kema is in traffic on her way home from the office, she calls Janice.

"Hey, Kema, how was the meeting? I have been waiting to hear from you all day."

"I formally accepted the position and will be moving upstairs to an office that overlooks Lake Michigan."

"I'm so proud of you!"

"The new position requires a lot of travel, so I may not be able to see you quite as often as I do now."

"Can you take me with you on some of these trips? You know I like traveling."

"Mama, I've never once heard you say that you like to travel."

"I can learn. You can't just leave me behind while you are out there traveling the world."

"Ok, Mama. I will see what I can do . . . The only sad part about taking this position is that Marsha said she didn't want to be my executive assistant in my new role."

"Is that right? Well, I have always said that the people that start with you may not continue with you. I'm so glad you didn't let the 50% share in your Daddy's clothing store stop from taking this position. Come over tonight so we can celebrate your promotion. I can fix us up some baked chicken and broccoli for dinner."

"Tonight, is not good. How about we celebrate together tomorrow night?"

"What? Do you have a date with that smooth-talking lawyer tonight or something?"

"No, Mama, I just need to unwind at home tonight. By myself."

"Ok. We can celebrate tomorrow."

Kema ends the call with her mother and starts thinking about when she told the reporter that the talent show would go on as planned. What was she thinking? How will she be able to help Janice and Darron finish preparing for the show now that she has accepted her new position? She will need a team just as talented as the team she assembled for the merger to help her get everything together in time for the talent and fashion show. Since most of her work at Resilient Financial occurs during the business week, Kema decides that preparing for the show will be her weekend side hustle. Hopefully, her new role won't involve traveling in the next two weeks. Kema is grateful that her father left her 50% of his store, and she will do her best to assist Linda with operating the store; however, she will let Linda know that she is not ready to purchase her share. Tears start to form in Kema's eyes as she begins thinking about her father. She wishes he was still here to share her joy in reaching her career goal and that they could work together to help uplift the community.

As soon as Kema parks her car in her condo's garage, her cell phone rings. She doesn't recognize the number but decides to answer anyway.

"Hello?"

"Hello, Kema, this is Victor. Did I catch you at a bad time?"

Kema's breathing stops for what seems like an eternity. Why would he be calling her out of the blue? "Hello Victor. No, it's not a bad time. I am just getting home."

"I was just calling to see how you were doing and to ask if you would be interested in having dinner with me sometime this week?"

Kema thinks, *Mama just mentioned this man a few minutes ago and now he is asking me out . . . Be cool.* "Sure, I am free for dinner this Thursday."

"Great, I will call you on Wednesday to finalize the time and location. I hope you enjoy your evening."

"Thank you, you too."

Kema ends the call and thinks, *I'm sure Daddy talked to Victor about his ideas for the show. I can ask Victor to join my planning team for Sweet Daddy's Fashions Fashion and Talent Show.*

Kema is at peace with this thought; she feels almost as if her father suggested it. She imagines Benjamin is looking down from heaven smiling and saying, "That's my baby girl."

ACKNOWLEDGEMENTS

I want to thank God for giving me the strength, creativity, courage, and discipline to complete this book. I am grateful to my mother, Willie Dorsett, for encouraging me to write this book when I told her the title. Ramy Vance, my coach at The Self-Publishing School, provided guidance and tools to produce this book. Annette Antoigue for listening to me read my first two chapters and providing feedback. Tyna Dao for carefully reviewing the versions of my book cover. My launch team for reviewing and promoting my book.

ABOUT THE AUTHOR

Shani Smith has been writing since the second grade when she received her first diary. She wrote her first book in 2019 entitled *I Didn't Part My Lips: Survival Strategies For Introverts Living In An Extroverted World*. Shani has a Master of Science in Chemistry and Master of Science in Cybersecurity Policy and Management. She lives in Maryland and enjoys reading, volunteering, dancing, cooking, and traveling.

Connect with Shani
Instagram @bookssjsmith

Thank you for reading my book! Your feedback is greatly appreciated. Please leave a review on **Amazon** letting me know your thoughts about the book.

www.ingramcontent.com/pod-product-compliance
Lightning Source LLC
Chambersburg PA
CBHW031844170626
46807CB00004B/1621